LEVELS

Fantastic and Macabre Stories
by
NATHAN SHUMATE

COLD FUSION
MEDIA

Published in print and ebook by Cold Fusion Media
http://www.coldfusionmedia.us

Table of Contents

Somewhere in Nebraska or Maybe Colorado

A decapitated zombie is actually good company—just the head, not the body. The way I figure it, when whatever it is brings them back, it's their meat and muscle that makes them mean. Maybe it hurts or something. Whatever it is, it's stronger than their brains, and they end up shuffling around and moaning without words and biting people, and that's nasty. But when you get rid of the whole rest of the body, then the head can be... not "normal," exactly, but it doesn't get all moany and chompy, and there's enough brainpower left that it can actually be well-behaved. I didn't figure all that out by myself, but I heard some and I guessed some. I'm good at figuring things out.

That's why I had two zombie heads strung on the back of my backpack to keep me company. Plus, they smelled like zombies, so other zombies—the moany chompy kind—mostly left me alone. Like I say, not the best traveling buddies, but every damned place in America smells like zombies now, practically, and anyway some days I can't smell them above myself. Candy was easy to tie on; she's got long hair, so I just tied that around one of the straps. Bud was a little harder, because he had short hair and was half-bald anyway. I finally discovered that ear cartilage is surprisingly strong, so I strung a rope through loops in both ears and put him up beside Candy. They're not the people I'd most want to travel with in the whole wide world, but they're someone to talk to, and since I could go weeks without seeing another living person—and then they'd shoot at me, like as not—it kept me from going crazy. At least as far as I can tell. They used to call me "Crazy Mary" sometimes. Now nobody called me anything except the heads, and they just called me "Mary," or sometimes just "Hey." I don't know what Bud and Candy's real names were; I guess coming back after you die kind of messes with your memories, or maybe it's having your head chopped off. So I named them, because I had to call them something.

I'd been slogging west across Nebraska, though I could have been into Colorado by now, or maybe even Wyoming, and it's been peaceful and quiet and boring. The roads were mostly still good, but walking on the asphalt day in and day out can be murder on the feet—and I was a waitress, so I know aching feet—so sometimes I liked to just cross some of the fields that are all going back to long grass. It was easy to imagine the buffalo coming back and covering the whole land from horizon to horizon with fuzzy brown, if there are any buffalo left to start having little buffaloes.

And Bud said, "Hey, Mary. Where are we?" His voice sounded like a grunt because he had no lungs, so he just grunted in the back of his throat. Candy did, too. I had closed up the bottoms of both their necks with tied-on plastic bags, and sometimes when the wind was blowing they sounded like kazoos, but I didn't do it for the sound; I just didn't want their crap smearing on my backpack.

Now, the answer hadn't changed in days, but Bud kept asking me. I think his brains were finally rotting. I just said, "We're in the late, great United States of America, Bud," and he thought on that. Or at least he shut up. Bud was more talkative than Candy. Candy only spoke when she had something to say.

Which was now, I guess. "Where we headed?" she said.

"West, like I told you," I said.

"We're already west. Gonna keep going until you hit the ocean?"

I didn't really want to answer, because where I wanted to go, that's a sincere thing, not just making conversation, and I didn't feel like discussing sincere things with a couple of dead heads. I was just thinking that, in all this land of robbers and raiders and the living dead and the dead dead, there'd got to be somebody somewhere who'd got their act together. Someone who didn't let themselves go to hell when the dead started rising. Me, my money was on Utah. Mormons out there, they knew how to come together and get things done. It'd been a couple of centuries since they wagon-trained it to the Rockies, but I bet they still knew how to keep their crap together and make life worth living. And if I had to join their religion to be a part of that, I was game.

But I didn't want to say all that because I might have honestly started crying when I realized I'm telling to a couple of rotting heads strung up on my backpack, so what I said instead is, "Hey—some of have to do the walking, and some of us have to breathe too, and all this talk ain't helping." So then they shut up, and I kept going west and a little bit south, keeping the road in sight but walking on the softer fields.

When the sun started setting ahead of us and getting in my eyes, I went back to the road, cutting off whole armfuls of dried grasses and weeds with my machete as I went. On the blacktop, where I wasn't going to start a huge prairie fire, I twisted the grass into ropes and started a little fire to warm up some ravioli left over from that morning's can. I had about four cans of food left, an unopened box of crackers that I sure hoped was still good, and about a quart of water.

I unhitched Bud and Candy from my pack and propped them up on the opposite side of the fire. Bud saw me take a swig of water and smacked what was left of his lips.

"My mouth is dry," he said.

"Yup. Has been for months, Bud. Ever since you died. Gonna be like that till you fall apart. You should be used to it by now."

He clacked his tongue around his mouth experimentally. His tongue looked like the leather tongue of my dad's old Sunday shoes.

Candy said, "Mary, can I talk to you a minute?"

I said sure and picked her up by the hair and walked farther from the fire where Bud was still clicking his tongue.

"Bud's getting stupid," Candy said.

"Yeah, I was afraid of that." Whatever brings the dead back and keeps them going for so long isn't permanent. The brain takes a while to go sour—the whole nervous system is like that, I think— but his was finally turning to pickle juice.

Candy said, "He's going blind, too."

"Really?" I said. "I hadn't noticed anything. How can you tell?"

"Sometimes we talk, he and I, when you're walking and don't want to talk to us. I notice things, and he can't see them."

For some reason, that struck me as funny: the two zombie heads, dangling from the back of my pack, shooting the breeze in grunts quiet enough that I can't hear 'em. It was funny, but I kept it all inside. Candy wouldn't have understood. Even with zombies that aren't moany and chompy, a sense of humor is one thing that just doesn't survive death too well. Believe me.

I took Candy back to the fire—just glowing bits of hay now— and stomped it all out, then unrolled my blanket on the shoulder of the road with all of the unburnt grass beneath it for padding, and Bud and Candy facing opposite directions on the road, keeping watch through the night because the dead don't sleep anyway. Though I guessed Bud wasn't going to do much good if Candy was right.

In the morning I didn't bother lighting a fire. One of the cans I had was peaches, so I opened that and ate half the can cold. It left my fingers sticky, and I could only spare an extra teaspoon of water to rinse them. I needed to find some more to drink soon, and real luxury would have been to have enough to wash my feet and my armpits and the back of my neck.

After I ate I crimped the can shut as best I could, rolled up my blanket, strung Bud and Candy back onto my backpack, and started off down the road, staying on the blacktop for a while just for variety. I'd been walking for a couple of hours straight down the yellow line when Candy said, "Mary, look to your right."

I looked, and I could see a few trees way out on the plain, and maybe between the trees I thought I could see a house.

"Damn. Good thing you saw that, or I would have trotted right by it."

Bud said, "What do you see?"

Candy ignored him and said, "I don't know if I can see a house or just an old barn, but the trees mean there might be water."

"I see it! I see it!" said Bud.

"You can't see anything, so shut up," said Candy.

So I left the road and hiked across country, through a couple of old tumbled-down barbed-wire fences, and maybe an hour later we got to the trees, and there *was* a house, with a couple of small barns and outbuildings around it. And the place looked good, like someone'd been keeping it up a little. There was a small corral or pen by one barn with no grass growing in it, and it smelled like sheep, although I didn't see any. Only one window in the two-story farm house was broken, and it'd been covered up with cardboard or something from the inside.

The trees had been planted long ago to separate the lawn from the fields, and I stood at the edge of the ring of trees and shouted, "Hello! Hello in there!" And then I listened for an answer. I wasn't impatient; if someone was living there, they could have been checking me out from an upstairs window, maybe even sighting me with a rifle, and I didn't want to do anything that would give anyone reason to decide against me.

After a few minutes I called again, and waited. And then I called a third time, and waited. And I figured that if anyone was going to hear me, they'd have heard me, so I started walking, slow and gentle, up the rutted dirt lane to the farm house.

I could see before I stepped onto the front porch that the door was wide open, and I started to lose some of my hope, because no-body but *nobody* in the world now leaves their front door open, no matter how far out in Nebraska or wherever they live. I got closer and I saw that the door had been locked from the inside with a heavy bolt and was pried open so hard that the bolt tore away part of the frame and bent it out so it couldn't close again. Someone had been living here up until recently, but someone else got in and took what they wanted. Raiders.

I don't blame raiders; everyone's got to do something to get by, and anybody holed up and hoarding what they can isn't being any more Christian than those that are out stealing what they need. If there ain't enough to go around, then there ain't no right or wrong in trying to get what you gotta have to live. I even tried to join up with some raiders a few months ago, but they laughed at me, this bunch of ex-cons and gangsters, and hit me and made me leave, even though I was the toughest damned truck stop waitress you ever seen. They never saw me the time I took down the meth head with the knife with nothing on my side but a coffee pot. Tied the poor kid into knots and had him begging for mercy without even breaking a sweat. That's why they called me "Crazy Mary" for a little while after that. Other folks wanted to call me "Mary Warrior Princess," but that one didn't stick; no princess had thighs like I had. They've slimmed down a lot since, though.

So raiders meant that the kitchen would probably be empty, and I was right. The cupboards had been cleaned out. But there was still furniture in the living room, including a chair that I swear was soft-er than any chair I'd ever sat in, before or after everything changed. I only meant to sit in it for a second, just to try it out, but it felt so good that I must have been there twenty minutes. I had slung my backpack on the floor before I sat, and Candy just watched me while Bud made retarded comments about the wallpaper.

When I realized that I was in danger of falling asleep I forced myself to get up, and went outside to see if there was a well or a pump. Right behind the house was a bright red pump set in a concrete slab almost hidden by long grass, and I almost cried when I heaved on the handle and water came out after only a few tries. I tried to get my mouth under while I pumped, but of course that's practically impossible with a long-handled pump, so I ran back inside to grab a bucket I had seen from the kitchen. I took it back outside, pumped the bucket full, and then lifted it up and had a good long drink from it, and then washed my hands and rubbed my wet hands all over my face. I may have been crying, or that may just have been the well water.

I took the bucket back inside, found the bathroom, put the plug in the tub, and dumped the water in. It took me six more trips to get enough water for a bath. I didn't care that it was cold; I enjoyed the shock of climbing in and sitting down. There wasn't a cloth or soap, so I just rinsed out one of my socks really good and used that to scrub every inch of my body I could reach. When I was done, the tub looked like it was full of old dishwater.

I got out, drained the tub, put some of my clothes back on, and took the bucket back out for another couple of fills. Then I took my clothes back off, put them in the water in the tub, and stomped on them, trying to work out some of the dirt and sweat. Then I wrapped myself up in my sleeping blanket—funny how I didn't want to be naked clear out in the middle of nowhere, and especially not in front of Bud and Candy—and took my wet clothes out to the back porch, where the sun was shining down. I stretched my clothes on the rail to dry.

Back in the house, I went upstairs and found one bed with a mattress on a bedframe, but no blankets. They might have been grabbed by the same raiders that took the food. It didn't matter. I lay down on the mattress in my sleeping blanket and sighed and felt weird and alien all over, like I didn't remember what it felt like anymore to be clean and lying down on something that wasn't dirt. It was only about noon, but I fell asleep right away and slept most of the afternoon.

When I got up my clothes were mostly dry, so I put them on then hauled my backpack onto the kitchen table so we could have a pow-wow without untying the heads.

"I think we can stay here until maybe tomorrow," I said. "But I don't want to push it. The raiders know about this place, so they could come back here if they need a place to stay or if they remember something else they want, or if they just want to fill up their water."

"Where are we, Mary?" said Bud.

"We're in farmhouse at the tail end of Nebraska or some damned state," I said.

"It'll probably be good for the night, then take some water and leave tomorrow," Candy agreed.

"I just wish I could carry the mattress with me," I said. "Maybe there's a small cart or a kids' wagon in the barns that I can take more stuff with me. At least it won't be so hard on my shoulders."

"I like the wallpaper," Bud said.

"We could ride in the wagon," Candy said. "I don't know how much we weigh, but I bet we get pretty heavy after twenty miles."

"You got that right," I said.

Bud said, "Where are we, Mary?"

Candy rolled her eyes, which is about the most hideous thing a zombie can do, and made me remember that if I hadn't cut her body away from her head, she'd be just as chompy and moany as all the rest of them.

I said, "We're in the late, great United States of America, Bud."

So I decided to check out the barns right then, grab anything good that was left behind, get it all together tonight, and then set out bright and early tomorrow. If I found a wagon, then the next thing I'd want is something to carry water in, because water's heavy and I could only carry so much on my back.

I was walking around the barns, checking them out before going inside, when I heard something like a whimper from the west side of the westernmost building. I pulled out my machete. It could have been nothing, it could have been a kitten, but it also could have been a person, or a dog—when they've gone feral, they're worse than all our bedtime stories about wolves.

I rounded the corner of the barn, where the sunset was starting to paint everything a burny color, and there he was: a man nailed to the side of the barn like he'd been crucified, except his feet weren't one on top of the other, they were spread out, so he looked like he'd been caught in the middle of a jumping jack. But there were nails through his feet, and nails through his wrists—huge ten-inch nails with wide rusty heads.

He saw me, and it took a couple of seconds before he could get his head to turn toward me. His eyes were as sunburned as his stubbly face, bright angry red that practically glowed in the sunset, and oily crusty gunk coated the edges of his eyelids. His lips were cracked like wax. I couldn't even hear any sound out of him, but I could tell the shapes his mouth was making: "Water." I had my water bottle slung around my neck—even here with the well, I would have felt naked to leave it behind—so I held it up and let him have a dribble and moisten his mouth, then another swallow that made him choke and cough.

"Please," he said. "Help me down. Tools... in there." He nodded back with his head to show the barn that he was nailed to. I went back around the corner toward the door. Then I stopped.

He had been put up there a day ago or maybe two, and the raiders who had done it probably hadn't gone far. Maybe they did it to punish him for not letting them in and making them rip his door off. Maybe he hurt one of them defending his house. Whatever the reason, they didn't just want to kill him, they wanted to punish him. And that most likely meant they'd be back, because most people want to see the results of what they do. How would they react if they came back and found him down? If he stayed here, they'd just kill him outright, or maybe torture him to death some other way without leaving. That wouldn't be a kindness, to get him off

13

the wall only to end up like that.

And he couldn't come with me. I don't mean I wouldn't let him, I mean he literally *couldn't*. They'd put nails through both hands and both feet. He wouldn't be able to walk; he'd probably be so sore he couldn't even be moved in a wagon, if I found one. And if I carted him away, and the raiders came back? I couldn't take a wagon across the fields to hide; I'd just be a sitting duck somewhere on the road, huffing and puffing as I pulled a helpless man and waited for the raiders to find me and give me hell for spoiling their fun.

Without going inside the barn, I went back to where he hung. He'd passed out. Maybe it was the effort of talking to me, or maybe he just relaxed from the relief of being discovered. I looked at his hands, swollen and blackened from where the nail punched through his wrists on out to the fingers. The veins stood out in an extra purple color, and the wound right around the nail was oozing with milky stuff. Two days hanging on a rusty nail had given him a whopping infection. Maybe something like this could have been cleared up before with penicillin and a tetanus shot, but now nothing could halt that kind of infection, not even chopping off his hands and cauterizing the wounds.

He must have noticed me there. He raised his head slow like there was an anvil strapped to it, and focused on me through his gummy eyes. His lips hung open like he wanted to ask a question.

I raised my machete and said, "Sorry."

In the morning, I rolled up my sleeping blanket off the mattress. I wanted to kiss the mattress goodbye, I'd miss it so much. Breakfast was the crackers, which were still good. I figured I might as well eat them when I was somewhere I could wash them down with as much water as I wanted.

I had taken Bud and Candy off the pack for the night, and now I carried them both out onto the porch and set them on the handrail. I turned Bud around so he was facing the trees and the empty sheep corral.

Then I went back in the kitchen, turned over a chair, and jumped on it until one of the legs came off.

Bud heard me come back outside and said, "Where are we, Mary?"

He didn't see me wind up and then hit him with the table leg as hard as I could. His skull split like a melon and spattered his sour brains all over the front lawn.

Candy said, "Better for him."

"Yeah."

I carried Candy back into the kitchen and tied her hair onto the backpack. Then I took the new head, threaded a rope through the holes I had cut in his ears, and strung him up beside Candy. I adjusted the old plastic bag I had tied around his neck stump to keep him from leaking blood.

"How's that?" I said. "Comfy? Any pain?"

He looked a little puzzled, like he wanted to shake his head but couldn't figure out how to do that without a body. Then his sunburned lips formed the word "No," but no sound came out. He hadn't learned yet how to have a voice without lungs.

I said, "I think I'll call you Danny. Danny, this is Candy."

Candy said, "Pleased to meet you."

Bookmobile Day

I sometimes misremembered what day it was, even forgot Sunday once in a while if I was busy with planting or harvest, but Maeve never let me forget Bookmobile Day, the fourth Tuesday of every month. She was always at my front door by nine o'clock or there-abouts, rain or shine, with her little plastic bag of two or three books she had read. She always said Thank you so much when I opened the door because I was her ride. Her husband Mike had the truck out by six A.M. and wasn't about to stay home late just so's his wife could get her silly novels switched out. Me, though, I was old enough that I didn't start work near so early anymore, and anyway I knew Maeve since she was a little girl, like enough to being my own daughter, so it wasn't no trouble driving her down off the mountain to Ben's Cross where the bookmobile stopped once a month.

She'd learned a long time ago that I wasn't interested in what she'd read since last Bookmobile Day, especially with the kind of books she chose, but there was always stuff to talk about on the way anyways, about her kids or her sister's kids or the weather and the crops. I always saw what she read anyway, though, because in my old pickup she'd take the books out of her plastic bag and look over their fronts and backs, like she was taking a last look at one of her kids before he went off to the factory in town or something. Most of the books had people like I've never seen in real life on the cover, men with long hair and no shirt and women with their bosoms pushed up to their chins. Half the time they were Scotsmen, the men, and all they were wearing was a kilt. Most of the people up here on the mountain are Scotch or Irish—in fact, most are Scotch *and* Irish after being in America this long and marrying each other —but I never seen a man like that in the flesh, all muscle and no fat. Most of us up here are carrying something up front over our belts except some real skinny folks like Cal Coogans, but he's an old old farmer who smokes like he can't breathe except through his pipe. I seen him without his shirt once, when I went by his place and it was laundry day, and he may be skinny but he ain't got muscles like on the books, just bones under his skin and weird hairs on the outside.

And the women on those books, they don't look decent to me; they're all slender like fourteen-year-olds, ain't yet had a baby or started putting on hips, but they're making eyes at those men like they're all grown up. We may be living out yonder up on the mountain, but we ain't like those hillbillies that marry their cousins at twelve years old. We're good Christian folk on the mountain. At least when we remember it's Sunday.

But I never ain't said anything to Maeve because them books is what keeps her happy, what with that big bear of a husband and her three kids. So if Scotsmen that don't look like no real men and women that don't look like grown-up women is what keeps her happy, then go for it, says I. And those ain't the only books she gets. Sometimes she gets a western, all hats and horses on the cover, and once or twice she's even got picture books, though she hasn't brought one home for a while, so I don't expect they went over real well with her kids or her Mike.

But this time we were chatting and the sun was shining for spring and she's all happy to get to Ben's Cross and the bookmobile's waiting for her—I mean, not just for her, there's three or four other people come every month, some even bring their kids, but still, she gets desperate worried when she gets down to the Cross and the bookmobile ain't there yet. Ben's Cross ain't a town, it's just a crossroads, one of 'em's even paved, and it's called that because Ben Chambers who was old when I was young, he set up a little grocery store there, and now his grandsons run it. The bookmobile parks in the dirt patch outside Ben's out of the way of the one gas pump, and Maeve runs on in like she's a little girl again.

I just take care of some business in Ben's and go back out to my truck to eat an apple and wait. Maeve's usually in there fifteen or twenty minutes which isn't enough time for a good nap, but I can just sit with my thoughts. If I weren't my own best company, I wouldn't have lived alone for the last forty years.

So this time when Maeve steps off the bookmobile, she's not as bouncy as she usually is. I don't mean something's wrong, but it's not as right as normal. She gets in and I start back up the mountain, listening to my transmission complain. Maeve just looks at her books like she's puzzled or something.

Everything okay in the bookmobile? I say.

She says, Yeah, they didn't have any more Louis Laymer books this time, so I got some other stuff. And it was a different lady this time, she said the normal lady's been sick a couple of weeks. The normal one knows what I like, but this new lady...

Maeve holds up a book, and I know the road well enough to look over at it while I'm driving. First thing I see is it's a hardcover, not like the paperbacks she always gets, and it's about half again as big as the paperbacks. The cover ain't got no art; it's dark green fabric, and the corners are banged up like it's been around a while.

I said, She wouldn't let you get what you like?

Oh no, I got some of them too, she said, and she held up the normal things she reads, all shirtless men and shameless women. But she said, When I said there weren't no more Louis Laymer books, she said I oughtta try out something different so's I don't run out of the stuff I already know I like. I guess that makes sense, don't it?

I nodded and said, And if you don't like a bookmobile book, it don't cost you nothing to stop reading it.

She says, Exactly. The lady said that reading puts new stuff in your head. I never thought of it that way, but sounds true enough, right? I mean, unless I read about it, I ain't never gonna see stuff like this on the mountain. She held up her paperbacks.

I say, Did I ever tell you I saw old Cal Coogans without his shirt, just like that?

Oh hush it, Joe, she laughs, you're gonna make me throw up all over your windshield.

I didn't see Maeve for a couple of weeks, but that ain't unusual. We're pretty close neighbors, about three-quarters of a mile, but I don't have much call to go that direction on our road, and if Maeve has call to come mine, she sure don't need to stop and say hi every time she goes by.

But anyways, it's a couple of weeks later, in the evening after I stopped work, and I'm out by the pump filling up a bucket to take in for the wash, and Maeve's middle child comes up. I can not re-member whether his name is Jerry or Jamie, I never have, but I know who he is anyway. And he says, Mister McDonnell, can you come up to the house and see my mom? I think she's sick.

I say, Where's your poppa at?

He says, He's still working at the fields across the valley and he don't get back till late, but Momma, she's acting like she's off or something. And I thought at first Jerry or Jamie was out of breath and trembly from running to my place, but now I can tell he's a lit-tle bit scared. This is his mother, after all.

I say, Is the other kids with her? And he says, Yesser, Rebecca sent me down to fetch you while she watches Momma.

So I set aside the bucket and say, Go ahead and get in my truck, we'll take the easy way up. So off we go in my truck, and it's getting pretty dark by the time I get to their house. Parts of their house is old, and parts isn't so much; it used to be a one-roomer, long before they got it, and it's just been added to, leanto on top of leanto.

I go in with him, and there's Rebecca standing by the door, all coltish and almost as tall as me but no flesh on her yet, and the baby girl's kinda standing behind her skirts, and Rebecca says, Thanks for coming, Mister McDonnell, and sorry for the trouble.

And I say, Where's your momma? because I figure she'll be lying down sick somewheres, but as soon as I say it I see Maeve coming out of the kitchen, just walking slow but not hurt or nothing, just humming to herself.

I'm confused, and I just look at her because she don't look sick at first glance, and I figure I'll ask her what's going on, but she doesn't even see me, she acts like, just wanders through the house humming some weird birdlike tune.

I say, Maeve? Everything okay? and she still doesn't say anything, just goes right on by like she's wandering through a stranger's house.

I look at the kids, and Rebecca's trying to look brave but it ain't working. I say, She been like this long? and Rebecca nods and says, She was making supper and then she dropped the knife and just started roaming like that. I say, She answer you when you talk to her? And she and the boy look at each other, and she says, No, and he says, It's not like words. I ask them what they mean, but they just shrug, like they don't know any other way to say it.

So I follow Maeve where she walked into her bedroom, I walk all slow and gentle so as not to startle her, just like they say you shouldn't startle someone who's sleepwalking, and I say, Maeve, it's Joe, wanna tell me what's going on? And still she doesn't answer, just hums that birdsong, all highs and lows and no real tune. So I say louder, Maeve, and I put a hand on her shoulder.

She turns around then and looks at me, and her eyes are like... like they're not hers. And she says something, but it don't sound like any kind of English, it don't sound like any kind of *speaking,* it's just sounds like they're coming from somewhere deep inside her. Then she tries to walk past me and I say, Stop it, Maeve, you're scaring the kids, and I hold her back with my hand on her shoulder.

And sudden she bares her teeth at me, and her eyes look like cat's eyes, and then she slumps to the ground, and I'm too old and slow to catch her so her chest and head bounce off the wood floor. But she's like she's out, so I tell the kids to come help me, and together we lift her onto her bed, while the youngest just stands in the corner and sniffles. And I'm starting to worry that something's gone wrong with her like a heart attack or a stroke, I heard they can even hit younger folks, but then she shakes her head slow and blinks and says, Joe, what you doing here, and why does my head hurt?

Well, the older two kids start crying, so I push them away to where the younger one is standing while I tell her what happened. And she's puzzled, because she says she didn't feel sick today at all, not even a headache. But she seems fine now except for a bruise on the forehead, so she gets off the bed and says, Kids, we better get hurrying on dinner, and Joe, won't you stay and eat?

I figure I might as well just to make sure everything's okay, so I stand out of the way while the kids help her get everything together and the table set. Right on the corner of the table is that book from the bookmobile, the hardcover, and she's using her bookmobile card for a bookmark so I can see she's into it some. I say, So's this book any good after all?

And she laughs from the kitchen and says, It's sure different. But it's a good different. And the lady was right, it sure does put stuff in my head.

I say, What kind of stuff? And she laughs again and says, You wanna know what's in a book, Joe, the best way is to read it. I can loan it to you when I'm done. But I say, Ain't read a book prob'ly ten years, don't wanna start now.

I eat with them all and watch the kids laugh and tease and forget what brought me here. Even Maeve acts like she's forgot. But I don't forget, and though I laugh with them all and eat hearty, I watch.

When I leave, it's full dark and Mike isn't back yet, but probably will be soon. Maeve's got a plate waiting in the oven to stay warm, and I wave goodbye and go out to my truck.

It can't be three days later that someone wakes me up pounding on my door. I don't wake up easy, but whoever's pounding ain't going away, so I yell something, pull on my trousers, and I don't grab my rifle but I make sure I know where it is.

Mike's standing there, chafed at how long it took me to open up.

I say, Ain't you usually gone working by this time? And he says, Gotta talk to you, Joe, it's about Maeve.

So I invite him in. I ain't got coffee or anything ready, of course, and I ain't rushing my morning just because I got a visitor. Mike and me, we don't get along too well. Never been an open quarrel or anything like that, but he's a big stern bear of a man, hair all over his body and a beard that starts near to his eyebrows, and he's got a sense of humor like a brown bear someone woke too early in the spring. I never seen why he went after Maeve, and I never seen why she said yes to him. Like I said, she's near enough to a daughter to me, so even after all these years I keep watching him to make sure he's keeping her happy.

Like I said, I got no coffee or anything to offer him, so I kick out a chair and sit down in my own. Go ahead, I'm listening, I say.

He says, You were up at my place this week?

I said, One of your kids came and got me because Maeve seemed sick, but she got better after I got there.

He says, Sick how? And I see he's not suspicious or angry, he's worried. So I tell him how Maeve was when I got there, and what happened. He grunts and says, Kids didn't tell me any of that, nor Maeve neither.

What's the matter now? I say. Is she wandering around again?

Yeah, but not quite, he says. I woke up in the night because I heard something outside, and she wasn't in bed. I look out the window and there she is, out back by the shed, lying in the grass and hollering. I go out to ask her what the holy hell she's doing, but it's like she didn't recognize me. She just grabbed at her hair and shouted things, nonsense things.

Like birdcall? I say.

He just looks at me strange and says, Hell, no. She's talking about fog and stars and what all I don't know, about books and old men and fish and... You shoulda heard her. It was like she was trying to say stuff she didn't know how to say. She said she's trying to talk it out of her head.

What he said gets me to remembering something so I say, Did she have a green book?

Mike looks at me even stranger and says, Damned right she did, on the grass with her, and she was rolling back and forth across it. When she finally stopped—she just up and passed out, and I picked her up and carried her in—I went back out and got the book. You know what it is?

I know Mike can't read more than his own name. I say, Just something she got from the bookmobile, I guess. She's at home right now?

He nods and says, She was sleeping when I left. I set Jamie to watching her close and not let her out of the house.

I said, I don't have a lot to do today, at least nothing I can't put off. You want me to take her down mountain to a doctor?

Mike says, I'd really appreciate that, Joe. I'm behind on my fields as it is, and I can't spare the day.

I say, Let me get some breakfast and then I'll come up your way and get her. Tell the kids I shouldn't be long.

He got up and shook my hand and went out and turned his truck around to go back up to his place. I dunked my head in a bucket and put on some clothes, made coffee and got some breakfast, and got all the way outside before I remembered that my truck couldn't go anywhere, least not right away. I'd had the radiator out working on it last night until I lost the daylight and had to leave it torn out. So I got back in there and wrestled with it and cursed and got it back in the truck just before noon—maybe no better than it was before I got it out, but at least no worse. And I finally drove up to their house.

When I got there, all three kids were sitting outside the front door, and they looked scared to death. As soon as I got out of the truck, I heard things from inside—thumping and stuff breaking, and caterwauling that I couldn't make out. I said, What happened? How long's she been like this? and Rebecca said, Right after break-fast, we were cleaning up and she was washing a knife and cut her finger, and all a sudden she just stuck the knife right through her hand. I tried to get the knife away from her—and Jamie said, I helped—and Rebecca said, and then she started screaming, I want it out, I want it out, and starts breaking stuff.

The baby was crying, her nose running down off her chin, and Maeve inside sounded hoarse like she'd been yelling for hours.

I got up close to the door. Maeve, I said, this is Joe, what's the matter? And something hit on the other side of the door like she'd thrown something, and she said, I want it out! I want all of them out!

I said, All the children are out, Maeve, what do you want out?

And she said, There's things in my head and I want them out, that book put things in my head, how do I get them out?

I say, What things? but she just screams for an answer, and it sounds like she's kicking and punching a wall. All I know is she's going to hurt herself bad, no matter what's wrong with her head, and I say, Maeve, cut it out, you're scaring your children, let me help you.

I start to tell her that I'll take her down mountain to a doctor, but there's a crash from inside and I know she can't hear me. I tell the kids to go get in my truck, far from the door, and I take a breath and then I open the front door and run in.

But it's quiet, and I think, That crash was the last thing I heard, like a window. And there's the window in the kitchen busted out and blood on the glass that's left because she climbed through. I get to the window and I can see her run into the toolshed out back. I'm not spry enough to follow her through the window, so I go back out through the front and around the house and to the toolshed.

The door on the toolshed is something Mike scrounged from an old house before it fell down, and the way it swings it's got a lock on the inside, and it's locked. I say, Maeve, open the door, ain't nothing that can help you in there, but I hear her crashing around with tools and what not, and then I hear her scream, and she keeps screaming, and there's something sounds wet, too.

Well, the door may be solid, but it's an old toolshed, so I find a gray board coming loose on the front beside the door and I start pulling, and slowly the old nail comes out of the old wood, the nail screeches like a cat, but even over that I can hear her screaming without a stop. My old arms ain't used to this, but I keep pulling and pulling, and finally the board pulls all the way out, so's I can reach in and grab the lock and finally get it open.

I open the door and Maeve's not screaming anymore, she's got her back to me and she's shaking like nothing I ever saw before. And I say Maeve? What you doing, Maeve?

And she says, What you said, Joe, and turns around, she's smiling, there's a bow saw in her hand, and the front part of her forehead's off, clean sawed off, there's blood all down her face, and I can see her brain where her head should be.

And she says, You said cut it out, Joe, so I am. The new things in my head from the book, I don't want 'em there, so I'm cutting them all out. All out, Joe, I'm cutting them all out.

An Eldritch Correspondence

March 23, 1932

Mr. Halward Comstock
c/o *Bizarre Tales*
New York, NY

Dear Mr. Comstock:
    I have written to the letters column of *Bizarre Tales* a number of times in praise of stories published in that magazine, yours and others, but this marks the first occasion in which I have directed my praise toward the author himself. I have to let you know that your tale "The Fiend-Haunted Forest" moved me like none in my memory. The conviction with which you infused your words with the blackness of infernal necromancy was sheer genius. I stand in admiration before your supernal talent, and christen myself a devotee of your works of the first order.

With admiration,
Mel Plowers

March 30, 1932

Mr. Mel Plowers
Madison, Wisconsin

Dear Mel,

Thank you for your overly kind words about my story. I rarely get notes directly from readers, and thus yours, forwarded to me by Miles Philo, editor of *Bizarre Tales*, is both a novelty and a boon to my spirit. I earnestly hope that my future tales, some of which are already queued up to be published in *Bizarre Tales*, continue to earn your admiration.

With gratitude,
Halward Comstock

———◆———

April 24, 1932

Dear Mr. Comstock:

Once again, you have exceeded my already lofty expectation with your latest in *Bizarre Tales*, "The Shadow Under the Mansion." Apart from your awe-inspiring command of the English language and your uncanny ability to impress the eerie atmosphere and scene upon your readers with an economy of words, I am staggered by the verisimilitude with which you ground your stories. Even when very little space is given to exposition, as in "Shadow," you leave the unignorable impression that these images are carved from a larger history of mankind's ill-fated encounters with a plausible yet mind-shattering pantheon of hideous realities.

I cannot help but muse that such realism has been gained by study and pondering, by an exquisite grasp of and insight into the basis of the legendary impulse within the human psyche. Please en-lighten me as to the path of your studies in this regard, as I desire to follow your hallowed footprints in plumbing the depths of the truth behind myth, for I firmly believe that in your fictions you are subtly introducing the insensible world to the shadows of truth for which they are unprepared to face head-on, in the full and uncompromising light of day.

In supplication,
Mel Plowers

———◆———

April 27, 1932

Dear Mel:

Again, glad that "Shadows Under the Mansion" struck a chord with you. *Bizarre Tales* is a magazine with an unimpressive circulation, and I know that within that readership, my own contributions are not commonly deemed favorites, so it is heartening to know that there is a fraction of that fractional readership which looks forward to my contributions.

Forgive me for not replying fully to your second paragraph, but to be honest, your handwriting is a bit too taxing to my weak eyes, and I have several tales in various stages of completion which demand my attention. Must feed the maw of *Bizarre Tales!*

Cordially,
Halward Comstock

———◆———

Mat 2 , 1936

Dear Mr. Comstock,

I undefrstand and fully agreee with your complaints about my penmanship; I was a sickly youth , and rarealy attended school during the years at which one is normally xxx drilled on ones letters (although my mother spent many hours teaching meto read at home, a task which alone qualifiesd her for sainthood). Do you X like my new typewriter? I purchased it in order to facilitate further communication with youX. My own words convey poorly enough the impressions and thoughts which I attempt to elucidate through correspondence, iwthout the added difficulty of my haphazard scribblings.

As I ewas saying, I wish to learn at your feet some of the hidden things which you have uncovered in your sturdies of the occult and mythic history of mankind, for I XXXX perceive that the frame-work in which you ground your weird stories is more than the creative happenstance with which lesser writers adorn their yarns for color and ornamentation. I know that epistolaryy conversation is a poor substitute for a face-to-face meeting of the minds, yet is it not enough to know that , in your tireles efforts to expand the mind of man in the margins of your tales, you have gained at least one acolXyte and apprentice?

I look forward to youre next missive eith eagerness.

Sincerely,
Mel Plowers

———◆———

May 11, 1932

Dear Mel,

You honestly purchased your typewriter for the express purpose of correspondence with me? I am flattered, and yet slightly disqui-eted; I never meant to be anyone's guru or prophet, and to have you attach as much importance to my "literary" output as you indicate is, to be frank, unsettling. I am but a lowly commercial writer, of little importance even in the field of popular fiction, much less in the greater and more impressive realms of literature. While I appreciate your friendly regard (bordering on devotion) for my stories, I would be both arrogant and dishonest if I did not indicate that work of much greater importance, artistry, and signifi-cance can be found easily, both in the stacks of your local lending library, and likely on the bookshelves of your own home.

As you now own a typewriter, however, I hope that you can avail yourself of education towards its operation, as indeed it is a useful contrivance, both for creative composition and for more industrious applications.

Yours,
Halward

———◆———

May 26, 1932

Dear Mr. Comstock,

Forgive me for the lag in my reply. I have delayed further correspondence until I acquired some sufficient mastery of the typewriter, and I think you can agree that my accuracy is much improved. I applied myself to practice by re-copying some works with which you are intimately familiar—your prior stories from *Bizarre Tales!* Specifically, "Oath of the Lurkers," "Spoor of the Moon-Thing," and "Beneath the Catacombs." Not only did those lengthy tales afford me much-needed practice with this unforgiving contraption, but I was also afforded the opportunity to commit to memory the spelling of the words "eldritch," "antediluvian" and "ichor." An education, on many levels!

I should have expected your *pro forma* attempts to dissuade me from my apprenticeship, for one must of course be sure that it is not swine before which one displays one's pearls. After all, how sincere is the acolyte who can be put off with a mere suggestion of other pursuits as being more worthy of his time? I would wager that the great majority of those who perceive something factual and concrete lying behind the vague hints in your fiction are thus redirected from their passing fancy, and thus continue to live out the lives of contented, if blind, common folk. I hope that my convivial but firm rejection of your attempts to thus dissuade me will be seen as a forthright sign that I am, indeed, worthy of such confidences as you might trust to paper and the post.

I must at this juncture congratulate you on your latest work published in *Bizarre Tales*, "Upon the Altars of Dead Gods." I perceive only vaguely, but still strongly, the gnosis which informs your tales of horror and dread, as one perhaps sees obscured shapes in those medieval paintings which were meant to convey sacred formulae to Templars and Freemasons but shut out the understanding of those whose lot it was not to understand. He who has ears, let him hear!

Now that, as demonstrated, my proficiency with this typewriter no longer admits to an impediment in the legibility of my correspondence, I hope fervently that said correspondence can yield fruit from the seeds which you have planted so surreptitiously in my mind.

Trustworthily yours,
Mel Plowers

June 1, 1932

Dear Mel,

I must tell you plainly: You are seeing things that are not there. Again, I find great flattery in the idea that you—and, presumably other readers to a greater or lesser degree—can find in my tales of shock and horror the impression of verisimilitude on which to hang a greater suspension of disbelief than one normally finds in "pulp" magazines. I thus find myself in the uneasy position of working against my own talents, such as they are, to disabuse you of your fond notions. The entities, cults, formulae, etc. in my tales are mere fancy and froth. As a youth I read copiously but shallowly in various eastern and western mythologies, and those half-remembered details, admixed and adulterated by childish misunderstanding and years of neglect, form the only documentary basis of the schema of lore upon which my stories are putatively based.

I say again, they are *not* real. I am not a church-going man, but

I would recommend that, if you must put your faith and efforts toward a mythology of supernature, it should of necessity be the one which has informed our civilization to good effect for two millennia rather than one borrowed piecemeal from stories scattered about on the newsstands.

Yours,
Halward

June 4, 1932

Dear Mr. Comstock,

Forgive me for following so hard upon the heels of my previous correspondence, but I am almost overcome with a triumph which will go uncomprehended by my family and neighbors. Through diligence, I have tracked down a copy, dog-eared and unfairly neglected, of the September 1926 issue of *Bizarre Tales*, which carried your first story for that vaunted periodical! I had to make several inquiries at those few newsstands in this city which carry *Bizarre Tales*—most apportion their space to such piffle as sports stories and motion picture gossip—until I could track down those individuals who habitually bought such fare, and at last persuade one to part with his own half-forgotten copy, at several times the original cover price! Your story in that issue, "Wanderlust of the Night Creatures," was like a missing piece of the occult puzzle which is forming in my psyche, and while I exulted upon acquiring said issue, I rejoiced all the more when I had read it and discovered the treasures of hidden knowledge it contained! I am now embarking on a mission to re-read all of your stories in those hallowed pages, in order of publication (unless you could recommend a more beneficial order in which to absorb them), the better to hold at once in my mind the disparate pieces of the greater tapestry which you are so meticulously constructing.

Your devotee,
Mel Plowers

P.S. Between finishing the above letter and posting it, I received your most recent reply. I of course sigh at the effort necessary to convince you of my discretion and maturity of mind so that I may be inducted into the secrets of which you only hint to the outside world, but at the same time I am heartened, for if you expend this much energy to repel all but the most determined and devoted of seekers, the prize awaiting the successful claimant must be all the greater!

I feel that I am on the verge of some great breakthrough, as if there were a wall across the mental vision of mankind which is, in my case, at last showing cracks. If my premonitions hold true, your next story for *Bizarre Tales* will contain the capstone of the edifice of knowledge, the prism through which all previous hints and fragments shall achieve full comprehension. Hasten the day!

M.P.

———◆———

June 9, 1932

Mel,

I have tried to be both honest and kind, but obviously the latter dulls the edge of the former, forcing me to dispense with kindness and be blunt.

THERE IS NO SECRET. There IS no hinted knowledge in my yarns for *Bizarre Tales*. I am simply an industrious writer, trying to make a precarious living by selling to various pulp magazines the stories they will publish. I write what I write for *Bizarre Tales* because that first story, "Wanderlust of the Night Creatures," was moderately well received by the editor and readership, and I try to be efficient by going back to the well repeatedly for more of the same until it runs dry.

Indeed, I am more than an industrious writer; I am what is branded a "hack." I write what I can sell, and what I sell, I write more. In addition to the stories cranked out for *Bizarre Tales*, I also contribute Western stories on a roughly monthly basis to *Frontier Adventures* under the name "Hal Stockman," and have also contributed several adventures of Dusty Donovan, two-fisted seaman, to *Fighting Adventure Tales* as "Stock Halliday." In lean times, I have even dabbled in the romance pulps, a genre to which I am not naturally inclined, to keep bread on my table; if you happen to come across stories by "Holly Stockworth" in last year's issues of *Romance For Brides*, you now know that they are mine.

As to the next story of mine to appear in *Bizarre Tales*, I abjure you with all the force that paper and post can transmit, DO NOT take that tale as a veiled instruction to you. It was written some months before I ever received your first letter forwarded by Miles Philo, and it was clattered out for one purpose, and one alone: to receive a check by return mail.

Please consider our correspondence over. Find another object of obsession, preferably one which welcomes the degree of slavish devotion which you proffer.

Hal

◦─◈─◦

June 9, 1932

Miles Philo, editor
Bizarre Tales

Dear Miles,

If memory serves, you have scheduled my story entitled "The Lone Sorcerer of Haggard Street" for the next issue of *Bizarre Tales* to be released. I do not know if you have retitled said manuscript, as you have done not infrequently in the past; it is the story about a lone magical practitioner whose secrets and power are stolen from him by an eager usurper through his torture and eventual dissection.

I understand that the production of the next issue is well underway, and I may already be too late, but if there is any way you can delay the publication of that story, I will be eternally grateful. In fact, I am happy to buy the story back from you to forestall its publication. At the very least, if you could publish it under a pseudonym, I would bless your and your progeny to the utmost generation.

Please reply as soon as possible to tell me what avenues are open to me.

Hal

———◆———

June 13, 1932

Hal Comstock
Providence, Rhode Island

Dear Hal,

Sorry, no can do. The issue's already at the printers—and far from being anonymous, you've got the cover!

Behind schedule, so I'll get back to you when I can.

Yours,
Miles

———◆———

June 26, 1932

Mrs. Ronald Comstock
Providence, Rhode Island

My Dear Mrs. Comstock,

My deepest and most shocked condolences to you on the violent death of your son Halward. While I never met Hal face to face, our business dealings over the past several years had blossomed into a true friendship, and I am saddened both by your loss and by the suddenness with which he was taken from us. I traffic in imagination as my profession, and yet it beggars even my imaination that such a promising creative life could have been cut short by a madman who can only be described as a deranged vivisectionist. I warrant that the poor wretch will be confined to Cairnford Asylum for the remainder of his days.

We have several of Hal's stories in inventory, by which I mean that we have accepted them and intend to publish them, but have not yet paid for them. I shall direct that such checks be directed to your attention.

I know that this is a tender and trying time, and I doubt you have given any thought to sorting Hal's effects. However, if you should discover any finished or semi-finished manuscripts among his papers, please send them to my attention and we will, if possible, publish them as well, with full payment to you. Hal was quickly becoming a favorite of our readership, and his work had drawn a small but devoted following.

Yours in sorrow,
Miles Philo
Bizarre Tales

The Burial of the Dead

Hanover reached under his left arm for the water bottle that hung from the side of his backpack, uncorked it, put it to his lips. A few drops of warm water trickled into his leathery mouth. Always a few drops. Never more, never less. He corked the bottle and replaced it.

Behind him Farris giggled. Hanover glanced back. Farris was grinning, letting his fingers crawl across his bald forehead like a fleshy tarantula. He muttered something, looked at his other hand hanging limp at his side, and giggled again.

Hanover left Farris to his own amusements and focused forward again, where the mountains lay jagged across the horizon. Their stark, fractal peaks, partially silhouetted by the sun, were burned into his retinas, tattooed in negative on the insides of his eyelids. They had never gotten any nearer, not after all his uncountable steps.

He tilted his head back to glance at the sun. Force of habit; the sun never changed position. It just hung there, about forty-five degrees up from the horizon, as if it had stalled and was stuck at that height until it would someday corrode away.

He brought his head down again so the brim of his hat would block the sun from his face. His feet trudged through the ruddy sand. Sand particles eddied around his boots, rebounded from his pant legs and chased each other off across the desert.

He walked. The moving sand made a dull electric moan. Dust collected in his nostrils, clotted at the corners of his mouth, caked his eyelashes.

Farris jogged up beside him, grinning, with his tongue caressing one side of his lower lip. He opened a fist to show Hanover the sand collected in his palm.

"Fear in a handful of dust," he slurred, and laughed like a whinnying horse as the wind piped up and blew the sand away.

It was later. With the sun stuck where it was, the only times were "now" and "later," and only stopped walking when Farris found food, which hadn't happened yet. Walking and walking, and suddenly the black woman was almost beside him. Her tracks said she had been walking to intercept him for a long time, but he hadn't noticed until she was almost close enough to reach out and touch with his left hand. Was that his north side? South? It depended on whether the sun were frozen in the morning or evening sky. It also didn't matter.

She watched Farris, who was walking backwards, windmilling his arms, then she fell into step beside Hanover. He kept watch on her out of the corner of his eye. She walked. He walked. Just two people—three, if Farris counted—going the same direction.

They passed a curled corner of metal sticking out of the sand. White paint had flaked off where it was bent, and rust striped the creases like a deeper shade of sand. The black woman stepped a few feet out of her path to kick at it. Drifted sand around it loosened enough for them to make out writing. 60 MILES/HOUR. The sign shuddered from her kicks, and the tip of the corner broke off and flipped over to embed itself straight up in the sand. Hanover watched without stopping. The woman caught up to him and matched his stride again.

Behind him, Hanover could hear Farris kicking at the sign and laughing.

Finally Farris started to hoot and caper in earnest. He jumped up and down, pointing at a spot in the sand that looked like every other spot they had passed all day. For the first time since the woman had joined them, Hanover stopped walking, and he touched her arm for her to stop, too. Farris got down on his hands and knees and began scooping away the sand. After digging down about a foot, he pulled up two tin cans. Small spots of rust blemished the metal, but they were still sealed. The labels, if there had ever been any, were long gone.

Hanover shrugged off his backpack and sat on the ground. The woman sat beside him. Hanover took his pocketknife from his pack and opened the first can that Farris threw to him. Baked beans, with a lump of fat that was supposed to be pork suspended in the gravy. He put it to his lips and swallowed a mouthful, then handed the can to the woman.

She took it. "I don't remember being hungry before," she said.

"You probably will be," he answered. "Because there's food."

He let her eat more from the first can as he opened the second one for Farris. Asparagus. Farris grabbed the can greedily and put it to his face. Green juice ran over his cheeks and down his neck, down past the collar of his shirt. When the juice had stopped running, he let the can down and looked into it. He smacked green lips.

"My, my, my," he said to the can.

Then he began digging out the mushy stalks with his fingers and stuffing them in his mouth.

Hanover turned to the woman. She handed back the bean can, now half-empty.

"My name's Celia," she said.

"I'm Hanover," he said. "This is Farris. He's crazy."

Farris giggled and saluted smartly to Celia; his fingers left a sticky green smudge on his brow.

After the food was finished and the cans reburied, Hanover undid the straps on his backpack. Farris wriggled his own bundle off his back, a folded dome tent. Hanover pulled a set of collapsible aluminum rods from his pack. Celia stood by as Hanover and Farris set up the tent.

"Where did you get the tent?" she asked.

"I don't know," Hanover said. He motioned her inside. She ducked through the flap. Farris followed her. Hanover paused, glancing at the sun. It was at about forty-five degrees, right where it had been at dinner, right where it had been when the girl had joined them, right where it had been as far back as he could remember.

Hanover and Farris stripped to the skin and lay on their clothes. Celia watched them, then did likewise.

Hanover slept. When he awoke, Celia was dressed again, sitting cross-legged, watching him. Farris was gone.

"Did you dream?" Celia asked.

It wasn't a question he would have thought to ask. He paused. "No," he said. "I don't think I ever do."

Celia shuddered. "For the longest time, I wondered if maybe this were all a dream. That I dreamed all of this whenever I slept, but while I was dreaming I couldn't remember the real world." She had been looking at the small drifts of sand that had come in through the leaking canvas while they slept, but now she looked at him.

"There is a real world, isn't there?" she asked.

He had no answer. Silently he stood up, shook the sand out of his clothes and started dressing. As he buttoned his shirt, Farris came in and extended his clenched fist. He opened it to reveal a lump of sand, molded by the moisture of his skin to the shape of his clenched palm. As Farris peered at it, the lump disintegrated until it was just a pile of sand in his hand.

"Fear in a handful of dust!" he cried triumphantly. Celia shuddered. Farris wagged a finger at her, grinning, then took his sand to the flap of the tent and blew it outside as if he were blowing the desert a kiss.

They packed away the tent into its two bundles. Celia and Hanover voided their bladders; Farris had simply wet his pants, and the blowing sand crusted his groin as they started walking toward the mountains, under the motionless sun.

"I'm hungry," Celia said as they walked.

Hanover nodded.

"I never remember being hungry before," she said. "I knew what hungry was, I think, but I didn't know that I had ever been hungry. Then I ate last night, for the first time that I can remember, and now I'm hungry again."

Hanover nodded again.

"How does Farris know where to find food?"

"I don't know."

"How long have you been together?"

"I don't know," Hanover answered patiently.

Celia shook her head. "I guess that was a stupid question. How could you know?" She was silent a moment. "Has Farris always been with you?"

Hanover walked a few more paces as he thought. "I don't think so," he said finally.

"Do you remember any time that he wasn't with you?"

"No."

Hanover and Celia walked slowly with measured paces. Farris ran in front of them a few feet, long hairs trailing gracefully off his head around his bald spot. He did an abortive somersault and land-ed flat on his back. He laughed, coughed, and spit through tight lips, spraying saliva back toward the other two as they approached.

"He's crazy," Hanover said.

"Why do you keep him with you?"

"I don't 'keep' him, any more than I keep you. He just comes. What should I do, hamstring him and leave him in the desert?"

There was no anger in Hanover's voice, only tired patience; he had thought the same thing before, he was sure—at least, it sounded familiar.

They walked past Farris, still spraying into the air like a beached whale.

"If it weren't for him," Celia said, "you wouldn't be hungry."

"I don't know that. What if I get rid of him, and then find out that I still get hungry, but there's no one to find food?"

She stayed quiet a long time after that.

Celia had no water bottle. Hanover offered his to her, but she refused it. "Not thirsty," she said. "Don't want to be."

After a forever of walking, Farris discovered food in his usual way. Four cans this time—two tuna, one tomato paste, one pineapple chunks. Farris ate the tomato paste; Hanover and Celia shared the rest.

"Do you ever save extra food?" Celia asked.

"No."

"Why?"

"Because I never have," said Hanover.

After undressing for sleep, Celia said, "Do you remember anything that isn't this?"

Hanover paused a long time before answering. He glanced at Farris, asleep with a vacant grin on his face. Was there anything else? Some part of him knew, or hoped, that there must have been something before this—but if so, the memory of it danced just beyond his recall, like the whispering sand skirting the edges of the tent.

By the time he finally answered, "No," Celia had already fallen asleep.

He watched her. She was fairly young—younger than old balding Farris was, that was sure. Younger than Hanover himself? He didn't know. He couldn't remember ever seeing his own face, and did that make any difference? He had been here forever; he was as old as the ever-distant mountains, as old as the static sun.

They woke, dressed, took down the tent and started walking.

Farris trotted up to Celia once they were underway and let a handful of sand trickle from one palm to the other.

"Fear in a handful of dust," he said. Celia immediately moved to the other side of Hanover, keeping him between Farris and herself. Farris didn't seem to mind; he hooted to himself and farted.

"Does he say that often?" Celia asked. "'Fear in a handful of dust'?"

Hanover shrugged. "Pretty often."

"It scares me," she said. "No, it doesn't—but it unsettles me. It's a line from a poem. But if can I remember it, it means I must have heard the poem somewhere, and I don't think it was here." Her brow furrowed in concentration. "It means something—the poem does. It's... The harder I try to remember, the more there's nothing in my memory to be remembered. It means... damn it, it—"

"It doesn't mean anything." For the first time since Celia had shown up, Hanover felt impatient—with her questions, with her questioning. From the reaction on her face, he knew his voice had carried his sharpness. "Nothing means anything. There's only the desert and the sun and a crazy drooling man who finds food. None of it means anything. It just is."

They walked in silence. The sun hung in the sky; the mountains fringed the horizon.

Under her breath, no louder than the whispering sand, Celia said, "I'm hungry. Again. Still. Damn it."

Later. Step after step after step, because there was nothing else to do. Toward the mountains, because it was as good as any other direction.

They came across a few loops of rusting barbed wire in the sand. Celia came across it, really—tripped on it and almost landed face down on it. Hanover caught her.

"Thanks," she said. He nodded and helped her extricate her ankle from it.

Farris knelt beside it, rubbing his chin in wonder. He gripped it between the barbs and gave it an experimental yank. It came up easily. He followed it a few yards, pulling it up through a few inches of sand. Then he dropped it, distracted by something interesting up his nose.

They started walking again.

Celia said, "Do you remember ever meeting anyone else, aside from Farris?"

"No," Hanover said impassively. All trace of his former outburst had vanished, buried in patience learned from the sands around him.

There was humor in Celia's voice as she spoke again. "Then you could say I'm the only woman in your life."

And for the first time since Celia had joined them, for the first time that he could remember, he smiled. "Yeah," he said, looking at her. "Yeah, I guess you could say that."

After supper, in the tent, as Hanover lay naked on top of his clothing and waited for sleep to slowly numb him, he noticed Celia watching him. She was lying on her side, her head resting on her arm, and as he looked at her dark naked body Hanover felt something he didn't remember ever feeling, but which he recognized as soon as it started to coalesce: desire.

Celia watched his face and nodded. She looked beyond him to Farris; Hanover followed her gaze. Farris was curled in the fetal position facing away from them, his breathing slow and regular.

Slowly Celia crept off her clothes and toward Hanover. He watched her, feeling an anticipation like nothing he could remember. For once, Celia seemed to have greater patience and control than he had; she slid her leg over him and knelt straddling his hips. Her dark skin, coated with dust, held the understated radiance of a dusk that Hanover knew he must have seen somewhere before, somewhere other than here, in a place where the sun actually goes down.

She inched herself down onto him until suddenly he entered her.

And there was nothing. Even as she began raising and lowering herself, Hanover could see in her eyes that she felt nothing more than he did. There was no sensation, none of that excruciating friction that built until it bridged the gap between anticipation and pleasure. Just the spark of desire deep in his chest that forced him to drive himself automatically up into her as she gripped his shoulders and forced herself downward.

For what seemed like eternity they went through the motions, feeling nothing more than the clear, thin ache that made them exert themselves against each other, until particles of sand crept between them where they were joined and began to chafe and cut.

Breathing heavily, Celia rolled off of him and onto her clothes, staring at the ceiling of the tent. Hanover could still feel it inside, the spark of desire, hard and distinct from whatever filled the rest of him, like the barbed wire coiling up out of the sand.

He glanced at Celia. She was still staring straight up, her eyes dry.

When Hanover awoke Farris was still asleep but Celia was gone. Hanover dressed and left the tent.

The motionless sun cast shadows in the footprints that headed back in the general direction from which they had come; Hanover could only see them for a few yards before they disappeared under freshly drifted sand. There was no one as far as he could see. She was gone.

Sand rearranged itself lazily around him. He stood there, watching the nearest footprint as the sand filled it in.

If he stopped eating the food that Farris found, would he stop being hungry? Or would that sense of appetite, once awakened, keep gnawing at him until it ate him alive? Celia had taken the gamble.

Farris stumbled out of the tent. He scooped up a handful of sand and let it trickle down onto the crown of his head. Then he shook himself like a wet dog and smiled a lopsided smile at Hanover.

At least she hadn't hamstrung them when she left.

Hanover started taking down the tent. The sun hung in front of them, waiting.

Party Favors

IVa.

I caught a pod to Lowtown that night and lingered in the space between two crumbling buildings, just outside the wire mesh fence that surrounded the platform. I was wearing my dark uni-mold again, and a black body sheet—not a very Lowtown outfit, but I expected it to keep me unnoticed, and therefore out of trouble.

Distant sounds reached me—barking or shouting, I couldn't tell. The air was caustic and almost visible with smoke and rot. I hung back in the shadows of the alley, trying not to breathe too deeply. The wildlife was loud, but not immediate; the tamer Lowtowners were presumably trying to bed down for the night, and the wilder ones didn't like the lights around the platform.

I kept my ears open as I waited.

I.

At the party on Broxton I had immediately been roped into earnest and trivial smalltalk by Allysia. She had recently had her ear redone; it was a graceful scallop-shell shape laid back against the side of her head, with ribs of reinforced ceramic and a lattice of gold thread connecting them like a spider's web. For all of her Edge affectations, Allysia was the ultimate bore, like a relic of old California that didn't follow it into the Pacific.

"But, really, how *could* they?" she was burbling, swinging her arms for expression as if she had forgotten the drink in her hand. "I'll allow, the Consortium has its problems, but for *anyone* to just up and secede, well..." She trailed away in a titter that she probably thought sounded superior; I heh-heh-heh-ed out of politeness and looked for somewhere to go.

Ronald, the host, sauntered by from the conversation he had just left, looking like he was open for another one. I flicked my eyes toward the door; in response Allysia automatically turned to see who was coming in (very nearly spilling her drink), and I scuttled off to Ronald's side.

"Ah, Hale," said he, as he saw from whom I was scuttling. She had turned back, seen I was gone, and immediately inserted herself into a nearby three-way conversation already in progress. "I see you've escaped her clutches."

"Just barely. Throb?"

"Let's."

We made our way through the clots of giggling, dancing, arguing people. As we skirted between hundreds of bodies to the throb table in the middle of the atrium, I watched the great kaleidoscope of the rich and Edge as they separated and rejoined into their many overlapping mini-cliques.

"Ah," Ronald said by way of announcement as we reached the table. I picked up a capsule and pressed it against my wrist, felt the slight pop, and then leaned against the table as full synesthesia gripped me for a split second. I could smell the pink light streaming through my head. Everything smelled, tasted, felt, sounded pink. My heartbeat looped back through my ears, reverberating in my sinuses.

I opened my eyes, not remembering that I'd closed them, and

saw the familiar pink border around my vision. The rhythm in my head toned down enough that I could hear the party sounds around me again. The music was throb also, with full subsonics thrumming along with the tone in my head. I dropped the empty capsule into a dish with several others.

Ronald still had his eyes closed; the vein in his temple was pulsing to the throb. He was a small round man; his face was getting that smooth look, like melted wax, from too many facelifts. There was a thin tattooed line down the straight of his nose. He was wearing a white ruffled shirt of flowered lace, and black net pants through which his red bikini briefs showed clearly, which was apparently the point.

He opened his eyes, sighed, and looked around. He nodded to me. I nodded back. He looked toward Allysia, who was alighting on group after group like a swallow, slowly making her way to the throb table. Fine strands of gold extended back over the edge of her redone ear and trailed after her. Her titter wafted across the room to us, even over the music in the air and in our veins.

"Honestly," said Ronald slowly, trying to hold his words together, "honestly, I don't know why we keep inviting her."

"Who's we?" I asked. "I thought *you* ran these parties."

"You know..." He flopped a hand all-inclusively at everyone around. "*We.*" He shook his head in dismay and scratched his groin through his pants. "She tries her hardest to be Edge, but it's all rancid. Did you know—" and here his voice took on a conspiratorial tone, "—that her father actually worked for a living? I mean, with his hands!"

"So do I, after a fashion."

He jumped a bit at that, then shook his head. "You're different, Hale. You perform services invaluable to the community. You're not Edge either, but at least you don't try to be something you're not. I mean, look at how you're dressed."

It was true. I was wearing a cool grey uni-molded second skin, so dark it was almost black, that covered everything south of my neck in one seamless piece. Very modern, and marginally trendy, perhaps, but hardly Edge.

"Do you resent it?" I asked.

"Not at all. Like I said, you're a valuable member of the community. You're like a rock, in counterpoint to all of these silly flowers growing around you." Again he gestured expansively.

"How artistic," said I.

Allysia's daughter Heaven came by and swooped up a capsule. She throbbed quicker than anyone I'd ever seen; within ten seconds she had fired it into her bloodstream, arched her back, opened her eyes dreamily, and pitched the empty capsule over my head into the dish.

"Ronald. Great party, as usual," she said with only the faintest trace of slur. Her eyes were half-shut, giving her a very seductive air. She was fashionably bald, with a two-inch sash of red silk looped across the top of her head and over her ears, tied under her chin.

"And hel-lo to you, Hale," she said as she traced her finger from my collarbone down the length of my front. Then she went back to the party, moving between people so gracefully she looked like she was swimming.

"Don't bother," said Ronald, guessing my train of thought. "You may be a respected member of the community, but you'd have to be a lot more Edge to have any chance with her."

I sighed and leaned back against the table.

"Aha!" Hands dropped on our shoulders from behind, and we turned to see Allysia, reaching over the table to us. She smirked at her own mischievousness.

"I can see what's on your mind, Hale!" she announced, with a wink. "She's fine bit of flesh, isn't she? Only the finest sperm went into her to begin with—and it's been that way ever since, I gather! If I was a man, I'd be wanting to slip it to her myself!"

She twirled off with a younger man in tow on her arm, and Ronald turned to me. "I don't suppose... that you'd do me a favor?

Encourage her not to come, for the good of the party?"

"How do you mean, 'favor'?"

He spread his hands. "Hale, Hale, are you really that selfish that you'd turn something like this—something you'd benefit from, too —into *business?*"

"Like I said, I work with my hands to earn a living—and without money, those hands are tied."

Ronald looked over his shoulder to where Allysia had found someone new to bore. "I suppose, with enough people here, I don't have to put up with her very much—and there's always throb, to take the edge off her..." His voice trailed off dejectedly as he walked away.

I remained, enjoying the music radiating outward from my skull, starting to feel the dryness in my throat that always follows throb.

IVb.

A screaming woman ran down my alley, blood dripping down her face and shreds of torn clothing trailing behind her. She favored one leg, and the three twelve-year-olds behind her were gaining. I faded back into the shadow of a boarded-up doorway in the wall behind me as they hooted and hollered by, mixing war-cries with descriptions of what they would do to her when they caught her, brandishing their broken-glass knives and kicking up the caked trash on the ground.

I hoped they wouldn't catch her—at least, not until she had rounded a corner, out of my field of vision.

A sparse rain started throwing heavy drops. I pulled up the hood of my body sheet to protect myself and pulled my arms up into my sleeves.

Across the alley from me, an old man that I had mistaken for part of the drift of garbage twitched as the acidic rain bit into his exposed skin. The small rats that had been nestled against his body scurried away, squeaking, as the old man dug through the trash he had been lying on for something to cover his head.

II.

After the next party, which I hadn't been able to attend, Ronald had vidded me.

"Hale, something's got to be done about that woman," he said. "She has all of the decorum of a Lowtowner."

I leaned back in my chair, studying Ronald's image. On the vid, he looked even smoother-skinned than in person. "Done something horrible, has she?"

"Yes! Well, no *one* thing—but you know how the woman is!" He anxiously waited until I nodded my head in agreement, or empathy, or something. "She fussed on about seceding colonies—"

"She was already onto that last time," I said.

"I know! She told everyone what she thought then, and told them all again this time, word for word! Then she went on with how beautiful her flowers are, and how long she works in her garden, as if everyone didn't already know that she's as automated as anything. And *then*," he poked his screen for emphasis, "she tried to tell Cornice that she was wrong about something to do with Neo-Contemp music—to Cornice! Probably the foremost authority on it on the planet, if not in the Consortium!"

I nodded placatingly, waiting for him to wind down, which he eventually did.

"Please," he said, "please just come to the next party. See for yourself."

"Ronald," I chided, "I'm of a dying breed: a Busy Man. And I—" I couldn't go any further; the pathos on his face would have melted any human heart.

"All right," I said. "Next one." And I snapped off the vid before he could drown me in declarations of gratitude.

IVc.

Something behind me moved. I jumped away from the boarded door as it opened inward and four older Lowtowners—maybe eighteen or so—sauntered out. Their patched-together clothing protected most of their skin from the rain, and their faces were so pocked with skin cancer that acid burns probably would have helped.

"Yo, *kisama!* You squat on our step?"

I backed up smoothly so they couldn't get behind me. "Just passing through."

"Hey, Tetsu!" one cried. "This *baka's* a Hightowner!"

The one he spoke to looked me up and down with a crooked grin. "*Hontō da!* A real, live one!"

"Hey, how long you think he be a live one?" said another, pulling out a knife with a genuine metal blade.

"Long as I want," I said. "Leave me alone."

Tetsu and the rest just chuckled. They all drew knives.

What the hell, I thought, and pulled my fryer out. At its discharge, the one who had first pulled his knife flew straight back through the air, crunched against the side of the doorway and fell into the darkness. The other three jumped back.

"He's dead," I said. "I have enough charges for you all. *Wakatta?*"

"*Wakatta'n'da,*" Tetsu answered for them all as they backpedaled a few steps, then slunk quickly out the far end of the alley.

III.

I was at the next party on Broxton, as were the usual crowd. Or so I thought at first; after some searching, I saw that Cornice wasn't there, and I kept hearing snatches of conversations recounting that whole episode from the last party.

Ronald stood by the throb table with drink in hand, wearing a zebra body sheet with transparent stripes. There were so many red dots on his wrist he looked like he'd been popping one every five minutes. He nodded to me, then pointed with his chin to where Allysia was regaling a group of four captive listeners with a story that she obviously found uproarious.

"What's she talking about tonight?" I asked as I picked up a capsule.

"She's telling the story from last time, about her and Cornice— *she* is! I've already seen two people leave tonight; my parties'll be ruined." He groaned like a man in torment.

I could see his predicament; there were, after all, plenty of parties in Hightown, and each loss to his was a gain to someone else's. Never mind that Ronald's Broxton parties had been the standard of comparison for Hightown parties, time out of mind; life was as ruthless and sudden here as it was in Lowtown in its own way.

"You couldn't just ask her not to come, or something as simple as that, could you?" I asked, twiddling the throb between my fingers.

"And have *that* get out?!" He stared at me as if I'd grown an extra eyeball. "If any sort of rumor even spreads that people get *uninvited* to my parties, it's all over!" His eyes pleaded with me.

I nodded absently, popped the throb, and faded to pink. When I came back, Heaven was standing in front of us, staring at me with an amused expression.

"If you're going to throb that hard, Hale, you ought to hold on to something," she said. Her head was uncovered tonight, but there was a giant blue spider painted on the crown, with legs running down almost to her ears. She reached past me to the throb bowl, lingering close just long enough for me to catch a good nose-full of the pheromonal soup she used for perfume. Then she popped the capsule, throbbed as quickly as always, and flicked the empty into the bowl. As she danced away she threw a wink over her shoulder at me.

"Why does she do that?" Ronald mused as I caught my breath.

"I don't know." Between the throb and the pheromones, I was

pretty fuzzy. "Maybe to show she's different from her mother—she can actually *attract* people."

"Humph. Speaking of her mother, let's get back to that; why don't you go and, ah, sample her company a bit?" Ronald nudged me with his elbow to get me going.

It took some control to keep from following the pheromone trail that I imagined I could still smell, but I managed it. I wended my way through the gyrating, small-talking, throbbing bodies, first to the drink table, and then until I found Allysia, who had moved on to fresh game.

"—so how could it really be any other way?" She twittered in derision at such people as would think that "it," whatever it was, could actually be some other way. She saw me join the small circle.

"Well, here's Hale!" she cried, throwing her arm around my shoulders. The gold tendrils from her ear tickled mine, and I almost spilled my drink as I jumped. "I was just saying, 'It's too bad that Hale wasn't here for the last party,' wasn't I, Joy?" Another woman, more restrained but still Edge, nodded on command.

"That's okay. I already heard."

"Oh, did you?" She frowned. "Well, I'm sure you didn't hear it like *I've* been telling it. That Cornice, she can be such a *snob*, don't you think she's such a *snob*, Hale?"

I grunted noncommittally and drained my drink. As she went on about how Cornice wouldn't know a composition from a commode, I saw Joy quietly slip out of the circle and make her way to the door. I stood silently and wished desperately for more throb until Allysia's story wound down and she looped her arm over some other newcomer.

"It's as bad as I said, isn't it?" asked Ronald as soon as I found him again.

"Yeah, pretty much," I admitted.

"And?"

"And what?"

"Can you help me?"

"I don't know. Can I?"

He sighed mournfully and reached inside his zebra sheet. From inside one of the opaque patches he drew a small catch-sealed envelope. I shook it slightly as I took it. Plastic rattled inside.

"Don't worry, it's generous," Ronald said. I put it into the pocket in my belt. "Just make sure she doesn't come to the next one, all right?"

"Sure." I clapped him on the arm and headed off for some much-needed throb.

IVd.

I watched Tetsu and his friends go, hoping I could leave soon myself, before they found enough courage to come back to test my claim about extra charges.

And, apparently, my wish was about to be granted. I heard the pod doors behind me open for the first time since I had stepped out onto the platform.

And then, music to my ears. I heard her voice, with no trace of superiority or even confidence for the first time, very timidly say—

"Um, hello?"

V.

The next day Heaven vidded me. "Oh, it's so awful!" she wailed.

"What is?" I leaned forward attentively.

She tried to go on but was caught by sobs. She had a silk sash tied under her chin again, but this one was an appropriate black. Even without her perfume in my nose, she was captivating.

"Mummy," she finally wheezed. "She got lost going to a party last night and... ended up in Lowtown."

"Say not!" I exclaimed. "Is she okay?"

"She's—she's—*dead!*" she bawled and pulled the black cloth sash from her head to wipe her eyes. Though it was endearing, I thought it all pretty theatrical; I knew I wasn't very high on her list of People To Call With Momentous News, so she had probably cried into her sash several times already. Like mother, like daughter. I played with a paperweight until she decided it was time to get hold of herself.

"The Watch just brought her up a couple of hours ago," she said, blinking and wiping her eyes. "The Lowtowners, they beat her, then killed her... They even stole her new ear!" She tried to burst out crying again, but her tear glands were apparently exhausted. She saw the futility of it, and went on with her message.

"The funeral is tomorrow night. You'll come, won't you? We're having it at Ronald's place." She smiled thinly, red-eyed. "It's somehow appropriate, don't you think?"

"Oh, indeed." More than you know. And maybe, I thought, there's an extra perk to all this. "What about you? Will you be all right, on your own?"

"Oh, I won't be alone." She dabbed again at her eyes perfunctorily. "I'll be staying with Ronald for a while, a few weeks at least, until life gets back to normal." She smiled again. "He's so Edge, and very sweet, too, isn't he?"

"Unh... hunh." Halfway through, I tried to turn my grunt into something positive-sounding; apparently it worked.

"I'm so sorry to have bothered you with this news."

"No bother. Anything that I can do for you..."

Her nod was perfectly polite, and it put that thought to rest. I snapped off and sat there in front of the vid, playing with my paperweight and thinking.

It had been simple, really. A false invitation to a nonexistent party was all it took. I had figured that Allysia, like too many Hightowners, didn't bother (or even know how) to read addresses, and depended on the pod to get her wherever she was going. And I had also counted on her overwhelming self-confidence to keep her from asking her increasingly-seedy fellow occupants of the pod where she was actually headed.

I fiddled with my new paperweight between my fingers. It was beautiful, really; a delicate scallop-shell shape, made of ceramic, laced with gold thread that tickled my fingers as I flipped it over and over.

Forbidden Aisles

The expected jingle of bells was not what announced Jim's entrance into the Asian goods store. It was instead a loud, hollow clacking sound. Jim looked up to see what looked like a mobile of bleached bone slats connected to the hinge of the door. *Huh—different,* Jim thought.

The store was dim, but still brighter than the deepening evening outside. At the counter to the left of the door, an old Oriental man with his hair brushed back from his face like Chairman Mao looked up from a Chinese newspaper and said something Jim didn't catch.

"Uh, hi," said Jim. "I'm looking for rice flour."

The man blinked at Jim.

"Rice flour?" Jim repeated.

The shopkeeper pointed further into the store, muttered something that sounded like it could have been "four," and went back to his newspaper.

"Right," said Jim to himself, and grabbed a hand-held shopping basket from a stack beside the door. At the Asian market he normally shopped at, he knew exactly where to find those few items Lily sent him for, but Lily hadn't called him until he was past that turnoff on the way home.

"But I need some rice flour for this recipe," Lily said.

"Well, if you want me to turn around..."

"No," Lily said petulantly. "Then you'll be late. Oh, I remember seeing a Chinese grocery in the strip mall south of the post office, the one with the German deli out front. You remember?"

He remembered the German deli at least, so he had found the strip mall, and sure enough, there was the entrance to South Sea Asian Grocerys & Goods at the very back where the pavement was cracked, between an empty storefront and a bookkeeping service with a hand-lettered sign. The grocery's name was the only English signage on the store; the rest looked like it was in at least six different scripts. *At least there won't be any complaints about the place not being authentic enough.*

Now Jim moved between narrow rows along crowded shelves. The signs above the aisles were in a language he didn't read, so he just counted four rows back and turned. There was another shopper in that aisle, a thin slumped man with copper-brown skin and a hawk-like nose, and the aisle was so narrow that even turning sideways Jim felt he had come as close to a homosexual encounter as he ever wanted to get. The man smelled of jasmine, car exhaust, and something tangy.

There were at least foodstuffs on the fourth aisle, though none of them looked like things that Jim would ever eat even on a dare. Front and center was a large section of duck eggs preserved in lye; the picture on the front of the cartons showed eggs marinated to a tarry black. That was one of the few products in front of him with English labeling on the package, though if the pictures on the boxes and cans on the shelves were to be believed, the contents of the containers ranged from bird's feet to an unfamiliar pink-white fruit to an old fisherman in a downeaster. Jim knew from experience that rice flour usually occupied space along with other powdered cooking ingredients; this looked like the wrong aisle entirely.

But at least it was a good place to start looking. The first three aisles he had passed were filled with porcelain bowl sets, electric fans, and various labor-saving appliances with young Asian women on the front of the boxes demonstrating their use. So he only had to work toward the back of the store to find what he was looking for.

The goods on the next aisle were at least dry; there were various noodles and flakes with stylized pictures of fish and crustaceans on the fronts. Among the few packages labeled in Roman characters, Jim saw some whoppers of Chinglish translation: "It's Very Goblin!" and "The Fruitcake Resides the Hole" were classics. He took pictures with his phone; who knows, they might end up on Engrish.com. No rice flour, though.

The next aisle was shadowy, falling between the widely spaced strips of fluorescent lights on the ceiling. *Back to jars again*, Jim thought, and though he could have written the aisle off and proceeded to the next one, his Chinglish discoveries made him stop and look at the contents of the jars. Again, fruits he couldn't identify were crammed into various colors of brine. He saw one squat jar that appeared to be full of sardines, all staring out with sightless eyes. Another was full of octopus tentacles, their suckers pressed up white against the glass. Something that looked like a jellyfish with eyes floated in tea-colored syrup, the only jar of its kind on the shelf. *Must be a local favorite*, Jim thought, and then did a double-take at the jar; he immediately chided himself for his foolishness because, even with the dim light as an excuse, there was no way the jellything's eyes had turned to look at him.

His browsing was taking longer than he had planned; he pulled out his phone to call and reassure Lily, but there were no bars. He grunted in disappointment and instead skimmed the shelves quickly before moving on to the next aisle—the penultimate one of the store.

As he rounded the corner of the aisle, he almost ran into the shopkeeper from the counter. The man looked at Jim with eyes that Jim couldn't help but think of as "inscrutable"; in this light, Jim could see nothing but black behind the man's eyelids. He was a full head shorter than Jim, and Jim felt himself bending at the waist to keep from towering over the man.

"You doing?" the shopkeeper said. He pointed his long finger —freakishly long, given his otherwise short, stubby shape—at Jim's phone.

"I was trying to call my girlfriend," Jim said. "But I can't get a signal in here."

"Signal is not for you," the shopkeeper said. He started past Jim, advancing back to the front counter. "Look a thing?"

"Yeah," said Jim, "rice flour. Remember? Rice flour?"

The finger pointed again toward the back of the store. Then the man was gone.

I guess I'll get home with the rice flour and *a story about the freaky-ass shop and its freaky-ass shopkeeper.*

He marched into the next aisle and stopped.

Every whispered cliché about Asian cuisine was made concrete in front of his eyes. Dried squid hung from hooks dangling from the ceiling, their papery tentacles rattling together like the bone chimes on the front door. Several burlap sacks sat on the floor, their bottoms soggy and purple from the fluids of whatever they held. A pig's head sealed in a layer of milky wax sat alone on its shelf like a bizarre trophy. A self-serve vat of some grainy white fluid sat open, and flies perched on the edges of the vat. The eye-level shelf was occupied by jars of fat locust-like insects, and as Jim gaped he saw the movement inside the jar; the bugs were alive.

"Jesus H..." he muttered as he felt his stomach flip over.

He backed up, then saw the storekeeper coming back down the aisle toward him. He carried a meat cleaver that was so large in his spidery hands it looked cartoonish.

"No shop here before, yes?" the shopkeeper said. He was smiling.

Jim backed into the final row. He felt cold air prickle the back of his neck and spun around.

The far wall was lined with coolers, and the coolers were full of meat. Labels in day-glo colors announced cuts and prices in a squiggly script he couldn't identify. The meat wasn't wrapped in cellophane on styrofoam trays, or even tied up in brown paper with white string. It simply sat on the wire racks in the coolers, dripping and congealing onto the meat below it. The white inner walls of the coolers were wiped with blood, and there was a deep red-purple pool at the bottom of each.

Most was just meat with bones protruding. But some was legs. And hands. And heads.

"No rice flour," said the shopkeeper behind him. Jim wanted to turn on the little man, overpower him, run like hell out of the store, but something behind his eyes felt too shocked and dazed. It was as if the cold from the coolers had seeped into his flesh, and all he could do was turn glacially to face the shopkeeper as the man pushed him with the hand not holding the cleaver. Jim stumbled back, directly into a two-foot space between two freezers hung with a split curtain.

"But you like butcher-block see, eh?" said the storekeeper through his smile. "Very popular!"

He pushed again, and Jim fell back through the curtains into darkness.

Love Among the Kryil

All right, then! Have all bellies been filled? Then let me turn my seat here, and you can all gather around. Yes, on the floor. Because I'm old, that's why! You have to earn these comforts, you know.

Well. This is a sight. I've never had all of my children and grand-children here at once. It is a blessing that both the cliffapples and the tubers were ready for harvest the same week, to bring you in from your scattered homes, and that Jondahl brought his whole family with him this year to deliver his summerpelts to market. I'll warrant that there's not a more favored man among all the Gron-dahr this night than I am!

Now, I've heard that some of you want to hear the story about how your grandmother and I came to be wed, with she a Kryil and all. I daresay that you have all heard the tale before, and most even from me on visits, but since you've never all heard it at once, I will repeat it once again.

Now remember, this was back before the Grondahr had broken the Kryil and they became the vanished and furtive savages they are today, hiding in distant caves or lurking under beds to snatch wicked children who won't sleep when bidden. Ha ha! No, they were then a fierce and depraved people, and made war with the

Grondahr continuously. All our young men back then had a duty to fight against the Kryil to keep them out of our lands and waters, to slay the men and redeem the women. They were, and are still, a devious and perverse lot. My own father taught me from the cradle never to trust a Kryil, and he afterward learned the lesson of his own words—he was captured on a raid, and to shame him the Kryil sent him back with his hands chopped off and his manhood split.

What's that? Speak up, Dahnale. What does "redeem the women" mean? Ah, the fullblood Kryil are a dark-skinned and dark-blooded people, and beyond all honor and decency. But you see, the virtues of a Grondahr are in his blood and seed, and so our duty was to find the Kryil women when we could, after killing or luring away their men, and to force our seed upon them so that, by chance, some children would spring up among the Kryil with Grondahr blood in their veins.

So now, back to the story. No, I hadn't forgotten. I'm old, but I'm not that old!

One summer's day, in the full flower of my youth, I was out with a raiding party, with our flints and our ironwood, and we chanced upon a Kryil camp. They were, I think, for trade with other Kryil rather than battle with the Grondahr, but that was no concern. We fell upon them to do our duty. And coming from one of the skin tents, that's when I first spied your grandmother. She had dark skin and straight black hair, like all of her kin, but her deep eyes sparkled and her red lips were parted in a gasp, and just the look of her shot a flint through my heart. Even among the fullblood Kryil, where no virtue or honor resided, there was still great beauty—I hadn't known until that day how great.

I chased her from the camp into the forest, and when I had caught her, I forced my seed upon her. But this time was different from other raids, for she herself was different. I faced her as I took her, and I looked into her eyes, and we even spoke some words to each other, I forget what. And by the time we were done, I was snared. And she, too, didn't fight like a Kryil woman normally did, not after a moment.

And afterward we sat there, in a natural bower of spring leaves, and I haltingly confessed my love for her. Yes, love. And she was timid, but she too finally admitted that she felt much the same as I. A love between Grondahr and Kryil? A strange thing, yes, but stranger things have happened, at least in legend.

Here now, Luhlani—no, I mean my daughter, not my grand-daughter, yes—your mother is making noise from her room. Go and see if you can quiet her, there's a girl.

The Kryil village to which your grandmother was bound was close at hand, and I knew that there would be many survivors of our raid on the camp, for we were outnumbered from the start and only used the element of surprise to harry the Kryil. I knew where the village was, and I knew also of a small, deep lake nearby, isolated by the hills. I told her of it and bid her to meet me there in two days, and she agreed. And so I left her, and rejoined my raiding part as we went back to Grondahr lands, and never said anything to them.

I was in love, with a strength of passion that only the young have, and so I had forgotten everything that my father had taught me about never trusting a Kryil, and everything I had learned on my own from the day of my birth. On the next day, without telling my father, I went to the temple and declared my marriage before sun and earth. Even when a man takes a Kryil to wife, such a declaration is unbreakable by man or woman or god or devil. I meant to meet her at the lake, you see, and surprise her with our marriage and take her as my own.

I swear, Luhlani, she's louder now than she was before! Take her some of the tubers from dinner, there's plenty left, and see if that will quiet her. Mash them well first, of course.

So on the morning agreed, I made my way to the lake and found her waiting for me. I was blinded and stupefied by my love, and forgot entirely that I was a warrior, otherwise I wouldn't have forgotten all of my woodcraft and been caught unawares.

You see, your grandmother had two brothers with whom she was traveling. They were suspicious, as are all those who are as devious as the Kryil, and followed her out to the lake. She swore afterward that she had not said anything to them, that they had come on their own without her knowledge, but of what worth are Kryil oaths? They fell upon me while I was distracted by her, and their first stroke gave me this scar on my arm that took forever to heal.

Your grandmother backed away as we fought. She knew not to plead with me for their lives, and of course she never pled with them for mine; they were all three Kryil. And though I had sworn love for your grandmother, that love didn't extend to these two Kryil roughs who snuck out of the bush at me.

But that first blood was the only blood they drew. I had forgotten what my father taught me about Kryil, maybe, but I had not forgotten that I was a fighting man of the Grondahr. Together I fought them, one against the two, and though the battle was as hard as any I have fought since, I beat first one and then the other, and didn't even look up to your grandmother until I had put my flint through the second one's throat.

And there I was, oathbound to my greatest love from among my greatest enemies. Why, I hadn't even told her yet that she was mine! But that oath is unbreakable, so I brought her back among the Grondahr and here she has been with me ever since.

Now. I will leave your bedding down to your parents, as that is one of the great freedoms of being a grandfather, and—eh? Speak up now, what? Here, can someone tell me what he said? He lisps so.

Oh, you ask, now that I had taken your grandmother to wife, if I have found my father to be wrong? So you're asking if I ever learned that I *can* trust a Kryil? Ha ha! Certainly not. I loved your grandmother, and I took her as mine, but I did not trust her. At least, not until I had cut off her hands and feet, gouged out her eyes and torn out her tongue.

Special Guest Stars

The beer dripped slowly now from the tipped can, leaving only a small remnant of Budweiser within. It had run down the arm of the easy chair into an alcoholic puddle collecting near his sneakered feet.

Beer, Sebastian thought. *Bleeding from the can, like blood from a wound.*

The glare of the television in the darkened room, reflected upside-down in the puddle of warming beer, gave him a double image of the dancing lights and glowing figures.

He felt his side. *Wet. Like beer.*

On the screen, the host with the perfect hair and perfect teeth (*I wonder if he ever had braces*) congratulated the Tibetan in front of a cheering audience; neon lights behind the host blinked out huge letters. Sebastian's eyes were slowing down; the glowing letters seemed to jump from shape to shape, dancing too quickly for him to catch their meaning.

The Tibetan looked like a refugee from a Fu Manchu movie. His stringy mustache hung limply past his pointed chin. His slit eyes roved from the smiling host to the audience and back. There was something strangely serene in his watchfulness.

Warm and wet. My side is warm and wet. Now my hand is warm and wet. And sticky. Maybe I should have watched channel 7.

As the host gestured, the Tibetan opened his flowery paisley robe (*at least, it looks like paisley*) and displayed the small red spot on the left side of his lean, tan abdomen. A tiny trickle of red rolled slothfully down to the waistband of his baggy burlap pants (*at least, it looks like burlap*). The crowd cheered harder.

Damn. What did I do wrong? I definitely should have watched PBS instead.

Camera number three pulled the smiling host into a close-up. "There you have it, ladies and gentlemen, the Lama Bu Gahhabi Do has just impaled himself with a steak knife—"

Big deal. Anyone can do that.

"—and is showing no ill effects."

Okay, that's the hard part.

Sebastian held up his hand in front of the screen. His skin was pale powder blue in the television's glow. The palm of his hand, the part that had been warm, wet and sticky (and which was now not quite so warm or wet, but still sticky) looked black. He focused past his fingers at the screen, where the host was flashing his perfect teeth at the home audience again.

"We warn you not to attempt this trick at home."

Sure. Sebastian tried to sit up straighter, as he was sliding down in the chair, but found that he couldn't quite summon the energy to heave himself upright.

Sure. NOW you tell me.

The Night Children

It was like something from one of the stories Mother used to tell me at bedtime, but in reverse. My mother stayed alive; it was my father, a hunter and mushroom gatherer, who coughed until blood trickled down his chin. Not long after we buried him, Mother welcomed Mr. Perce to our home on the edge of the forest and to her bed. I did not blame her for marrying again, because a woman alone is a fragile thing; instead I blamed Mr. Perce for pressing his case so energetically in her time of weakness. He may have filled an emptiness in our life and our little house, but he filled it with a stinking cancer that smelled of dead fish.

My older sister Lydia had an escape; when she saw that Mr. Perce was a cruel serpent of a man, she half-corralled Jim Olandt into marrying her just so she could escape the shadow which now filled our home on the edge of the wood. I would have liked to escape with her, but the tiny new house Jim made for her had no room in it for me, and anyway, Mr. Perce wouldn't have let me go. He liked having gotten a son old enough to do chores without waiting through the years of squalling infancy, even though I was barely big enough to wrestle the bucket back from the well. In that chore, as in all others, he waited for me to make any mistake he could punish me for; a slop of water just inside the doorjamb was enough for him to remove his belt with relish. After the first time, when Mother got her own black eye for getting in the way, she never tried to defend me again.

Mr. Perce was a fisherman. He left every morning before the sun rose and was back stinking of fish before supper, or sometimes of fish and liquor after supper. Every time I saw a dark cloud on the ocean horizon at daybreak, I prayed that this would be the one that swept him overboard and sent him to his darling fishes. At first I confessed the sin of such dark thoughts regularly, until I realized that I couldn't repent to the priest of prayers I which made in all sincerity and which I had no intention of ceasing. So instead I stopped confessing them.

I had thought myself too old for bedtime stories until Father died, but afterward, with Mother and myself stuck alone in that home which now reeked of the invader, I longed for them. Of course, solely because they were a comfort to me, Mr. Perce forbade them. But sometimes, when he decided that the lure of strong drink was worth more than the lure of my mother's bed until late at night, there was time for her to sit on the edge of my pallet and tell me tales as she had told years before. I never asked her to change the wicked stepmothers in the stories into stepfathers, but maybe she knew I was silently making that substitution.

My favorite stories were of the Night Children, because Father had said that he had seen them once, having misjudged the time and lost his way in the dark in the great forest that abutted our house. In the old stories they were like plump infants, cherubs of golden hair and bright eyes and (in some stories) miniature wings who came out and danced in the forest after the fall of night, and who waylaid errant travelers not out of wickedness but out of thoughtless mischievousness. Father's story of seeing the Night Children was not polished by long years of telling as Mother's stories were, and he was a man of halting speech, but his recounted glimpses of them—a glint of bright hair, a whisper of irrepressible laughter—lent new magic to all of Mother's tales of long ago and far away, because the magic was that much more real.

Then the fishing season ended, and Mr. Perce stayed always at home, except when the public house called to him. I fantasized about building my own room onto the side of Lydia's house so I would have somewhere to run away to. I dreamt that it was summer again, the season for accidents at sea, and woke in disappointment to find autumn barely beginning. I spent far too much of my time daydreaming about how and when to escape Mr. Perce. And yet, it was he that finally separated us, not I.

Late one evening when he had not vacated the house for the inn and was thus in a sober, terrible mood, he instructed me to stir up the fire and throw some logs on to keep the house warm for the night. I was about to go to bed myself, and so I set about the task in haste—too much haste, for as I stirred the ashes, a hot ember popped and leapt from the fireplace and landed on Mr. Perce's bare foot.

He cursed with words that any God-fearing man would be ashamed to say in front of his wife, and aimed a blow at my head. And I committed the cardinal sin in Mr. Perce's eyes: I ducked and stepped away.

Both his eyes and his face turned red, and spittle flew from his lips as he promised that my days in that house were over. I tried to scamper around him to get away, but he caught my shoulders, and with the strength of a man who spends his days throwing sodden nets to and from the deck, he bore me to the door, heaved me out, and locked the door behind me before I even landed on my shoulder.

I sat up, too stunned to cry. All was silent inside the house, save for something that I took to be my mother's soft sobs in the corner, still afraid or unwilling to cross her husband. This was not how I had fantasized my escape, here in the cold of the night with nothing except the clothes I wore, without even shoes or socks on my feet, and a bruise growing on my shoulder. I picked myself up, straightened my torn-aside shirt, and was about to retreat to the warmth of the small stable where our workhorse and cats lived, when Mr. Perce's voice came booming through the door: "And let me not catch ye in the stable, for I'll come out a' midnight, and if I catch ye I'll skin ye!"

I stopped and considered my options in despair. Our house was far from town and close to the woods, and trekking to any friendly neighbor—if there were any whom Mr. Perce had not already thrust away—would mean stumbling through the moonless night with no shoes. The sky was chill above me, as if the stars were sucking out the warmth left in the earth by the sun, and the dew was already settling. If I headed under the trees, at least, I would have some protection from the dew and any wind that might spring up, and surely it could scarcely be darker under the trees than under the sky. I therefore set my shoulders as bravely as I could and took the close path into the woods, the first time I had ventured thus at night.

It seemed an eternity of stubbed toes and scratched forearms later, but it was probably less than two hundred yards, when I finally collapsed in the welled roots of some enormous tree. I had nowhere to go, at least until morning; I had no need to go farther into the forest, nor was I certain that I would know my directions out in the morning if I did. The space around the roots was thick and soft with many years' worth of spongy moss, at least as soft as my straw pallet at home had ever been. I tore up some of the moss, curled into the depression thus made, and covered myself as well as I could with the moss I had pulled out, making a crude quilt of what the forest provided. I had thought I would stay awake for hours, listening to the forest breathe and dwelling on the injustice that had suddenly made me as good as an orphan, but now that the night air had cooled my shock and anger, I went to sleep without expecting it.

When I awoke hours later, the moon had risen and was peeking through a break in the forest canopy, its rays practically at my feet. Everything in this little corner of forest was outlined with silvery moonlight. And I scarcely had time to wonder what had brought me awake when I saw the Night Children.

They, too, were glazed in silver from the moon. They crept through the forest with the natural stealth that all forest animals have, and a twittering sound, almost like laughter, passed from one to another. There were two I could see clearly, though there may well have been others outside the small pool of reflected light. I didn't dare breathe and felt the incredible volume of my pounding heart as I looked without blinking on a bedtime story come to life.

They were as they had been described by Mother, and yet unlike. Their hair was not of golden tresses; it was pale and colorless, and stood out in shocks. They were not plump like cherubim, but pudgy and bloated with yet a hardness underneath, like a wallowing hog. Their noses were like a hog's too, upturned and wide, and they cocked their heads with brittle motions as first one, then another, tittered in a voice more like a mockingbird's than a delighted child's.

The one in front wagged his head back and forth toward where I was concealed, and as he stepped into the moonlight I saw that his eyes were small and completely white. He was blind! They all were. Their keen noses, and their wide ears that I saw now beneath their hair, wide and swept back like bats' wings, compensated for their blindness, and they could roam the forest as well as any hunting owl.

The lead one sniffed again, and I realized that he had scented me. It did me no good to cower under a covering of moss, for the darkness could not hide me. I stood, dumping the mossy clumps to the ground.

He came forward, this bold one, until he stood an arm's length from me. He was perhaps my height, though he seemed shorter because his legs were bent in a perpetual crouch as if ready to spring away at any time. He sniffed, and sniffed again, and cocked his head as if confused.

And somehow I knew that covering myself in moss had disguised my human scent, at least enough to bewilder his senses. I smelled alien, yet I also smelled of the forest.

He reached out a hand toward me, the fingers long and slender, the ends thin and calloused into points as strong as any blunt talon. Not knowing what else to do, I did likewise until my fingertips touched his. He grasped and felt my hand, then turned his head toward his shoulder and made their giggling call back toward his companions, and I saw for the first time the thicket of pointed teeth that crowded his mouth. Then he drew me forward, not as a cap-tive, but as a companion, and together we joined the others. There were now three other Night Children, and as they tittered to each other, I joined in, giggling in honest relief. They meant me no mal-ice; they had accepted me as one of them.

We stayed the night in the forest, running and darting between the trees and bracken, them navigating by their hearing and smell and touch, I darting between patches of isolated moonlight. They stripped the hard skin from a reedy plant that grew by a marshy stream and sucked the marrow-like core; I did as well, finding the taste bland but wild. They led me to a wild crabapple tree, and I chewed the sour fruit until my jaw was sore before it was pulped enough to swallow. This was how they survived in the forest at night, and they were teaching me how to live like one of them.

There was one spot in the forest where they reared back and gave a wide berth to something almost buried in leaves. They cir-cled it, sniffing and baring their teeth, and one or two of them hissed at it in something like a show of bravery. I stared at it until the filtered moonlight showed me enough detail to identify it: a worn leather glove, lost in the forest who knows how many months or years before. It might even have belonged to my father.

I saw them once all go quiet together, and then leap as one on something in the bushes. Their quarry might have been a squirrel or some other rodent; I didn't see it until eight hands had grasped it and torn it apart, red flesh in their fingers that went immediately into their mouths.

Toward dawn, they led me to a lair hollowed into the bole of an enormous fallen tree. They packed themselves and me in there together like mice in their nest and settled to sleep as the lightening sky showed through the canopy overhead. I was tired to my bones, but I lay awake as they slept, the head of the nearest one nestled on my shoulder.

Were they my new family? Surely they would recognize eventually that I was not one of them; would their acceptance of me have become unbreakable by the time my otherness, my humanity, became apparent to them? Even with the scent of the moss still lingering on me, they had to know, cooped tightly in this burrow, that I was not like them.

I thought of their night jaunt—full of playful activity it seemed, and yet almost all their activities centered around finding food, and that was a fairly meager harvest; the crabapples on that one tree wouldn't last forever. Were their bloated bellies the natural consequence of fattening up for the lean winter ahead? I had precious little fat on my body; I couldn't live on what was to be found in the forest in winter, even if I could survive without freezing to death.

I thought of the little cottage on the edge of the forest, where the coals of the fire still glowed sleepily, waiting for someone to stir them to blazing life again. I thought of the larder, stocked with plain but substantial food for the winter.

I wondered how hungry the Night Children would get for meat, once the squirrels had all hidden themselves away until spring.

I wondered if they would have an appetite for human meat that smelled like fish.

On the Demise of Rory Calloran

July 9th, 1863

The good Father Kettrick has supplied me with this foolscap and pencil, and further agreed to forebear the redemption of my soul and instead to give me solitude for my final hour. I think that this evidence of my literacy has shocked the poor clergyman into acquiescence. I shall therefore attempt to explain for the benefit of those still baffled by the mystery leading to my conviction the circumstances, largely of my own doing, which lead me to this, the very shadow of the gallows. I shall present it in the form of a story, so that those who have not already heard my whispered and unbelievable claims will not be hopelessly confused at the outset.

Rory Calloran was born into a family of means, and discovered as he matured both the blessings of his station and the limits of material blessings. He was a quick and studious boy, but only a few years into his primary school education he discovered that his body was not the equal of his mind. By the time he was twelve years old, he was forced to walk with a cane. Prior to his matriculation into university, the cane had become two crutches. His diploma, with honors, was received when his strength had degenerated to the point where the crutches were at times supplanted by a wheeled chair in the hands of one of his household staff. His parents had used both money and influence to secure the advice and attentions of those in the top echelon of medical achievement, but this congenital wasting was not something they could halt or even concretely diagnose; it was, in the words of one practitioner, a "defect in the germ," and as such could not be corrected without supplanting God Himself. He would never be a husband and father, nor would he ever inherit from his own father the management of the family estate and holdings. At most, young Rory could be made comfortable, and the household could anticipate the needs of his impending helplessness in all personal matters within the next decade.

But as I have said, Rory Calloran was studious and intellectual, perhaps more so owing to the imbalance between mind and body. He was aware from an early age that even as he enriched and expanded his brain, the fragile body from which it drew its sustenance would continually degenerate until he was left imprisoned in a withered husk. And thus it was also from an early age that he turned his greatest resource, his mind, to the solution of his overshadowing doom.

Owing to both the university library's impressive holdings of antiquarian books and manuscripts and the Calloran family's history of considerable financial support to said institution, Rory was allowed to explore the dusty stacks to his heart's content, far beyond the liberty accorded to his fellow students. Accompanied by his Negro servants, who were entirely illiterate and thus could not report back any unease stemming from the nature of his self-directed studies, Rory made himself the master of the library's holdings beyond the mastery of any of the librarians paid to maintain the collection. He plumbed storerooms in which the contents had been stored uncatalogued for years beyond counting, ostensibly waiting for a resource of expertise among the staff which such specialized curation would require, but in actuality neglected because those few of the staff who had ever known what those holdings included had shrunk from intimate contact with such questionable materials.

Questionable? In truth, there is little question about the knowledge Rory found, for tucked into the far corners of the library's vaults and basements, hidden by dust and willful ignorance, were codices and manuscripts containing the heterodox wisdom of ancient fraternities and cults, caretakers of mouldering knowledge handed down with sacred care by lineal brotherhoods stretching back to the dimmest reaches of human antiquity, back to aeons so far removed from the prosaic nature of modern human experience that intimations of congress between the sons of men and denizens of other realms—be they divine, infernal, or beyond such definitions entirely—seemed somehow plausible. For Rory had seen the limits of the paltry knowledge amassed by the scientific men of this scientific age, and was thus prepared to transplant his faith to that knowledge bequeathed to an earlier age of mankind by beings beyond the ken of the plodding advances of those so-called men of science.

Having studied in those library vaults for all the years of his university education, it was still four months past his graduation before he finally felt expert enough to undertake the enterprise whose execution had suggested itself to him in those worm-eaten volumes. He first called the family solicitor and swore him to secrecy about the work which he was about to perform. The solicitor begged and pleaded not to be pressed into service, but Rory had in his possession documentary proof of a dalliance which the solicitor had unwisely undertaken, and inasmuch as the solicitor's holdings and community standing came from the family into which he was married, he was constrained to assist, however reluctantly. The document Rory had the solicitor draw up was a Will of sorts; it codified the transfer of all of Rory's theretofore-received inheritance, including the trust from which he drew his sizable livelihood, and all rights to the considerable additional estate he would receive upon his parents' demise, to... He left the name blank, but had the Will recognize as valid the future declaration of transferee in a separate document to be filed later.

With the legal paperwork prepared, Rory had his servant take him to the common jails of the city, perusing those being held for various infractions and charges. Both his community standing and his generosity with funds to those holding the keys allowed him access of a kind not casually bestowed, and Rory reflected on the fact that his material resources were, indeed, a kind of compensation for the ill blow of fortune struck him in the degenerative malady which was so intrinsically a part of his mortal flesh. He perused those poor unfortunates, mostly of squalid upbringing and intemperate natures, whose ill-advised habitual actions had landed them in the grimy holding cells of several precincts, searching for one who was suitable for his schemes.

At last, he found one Thomas O'Brien sleeping under a stinking blanket in the back cell of the police precinct in one of the more degenerate parts of the city, a neighborhood so fouled by its tenement-dwelling denizens that his Negro manservant had gone to the limits of servile propriety and somewhat beyond to dissuade him from visiting there. But Rory would not be dissuaded, and O'Brien was the reward for his perseverance. He was a strapping lad in his early twenties, broad of shoulder and square of jaw; Rory, who had spent most of his life envying able-bodied young men in their prime, could see that despite his ancestry of criminal and destitute immigrants, his physical frame was as yet unmarred by the dissolution to which those in his station were inevitably heir.

With the commanding officer Rory then reviewed O'Brien's criminal record. O'Brien was not an habitual drunkard, though more from a robust ability to hold his liquor than any tendency toward temperance. He was known to the police for frequent brawling and other forms of violence; in fact, his current imprisonment was the consequence of his having beaten severely a prostitute the night before. The police were not as concerned for the well-being of the prostitute as they would have been for that of a woman of virtue, though, and with Rory's offer to pay O'Brien's outstanding charges and an additional honorarium to compensate the officers for the irregularity, the officer was agreeable to releasing O'Brien directly into Rory's custody.

Conversing with O'Brien as little as possible, Rory had his man-servant bring him to their carriage and thus back to Rory's apartments in the family estate which, in deference to Rory's maturity, his parents had arranged with separate entrances. Rory brought O'Brien, still manacled as he had been on leaving the precinct, into the parlor of his apartments, which he had cleared of furnishing in preparation for this event.

Already drawn on the floor was a crawling circular diagram painted in a paste made from the ashes of burnt goats, scrawled by Rory himself on his hands and knees after a pattern shown on an old manuscript written on crumbling papyrus. He had his manservant lead the bewildered O'Brien, who had said very little of the events since leaving his cell because of the effects of confusion on his uncultured brain, to a chair in the center of the maelstrom of weird characters on the floor, after which Rory dismissed the man-servant and instructed him to lock the door on his exit. It was with, I think, mingled trepidation and relief that the servant left the prepared room.

Using his crutches for mobility, Rory first seated himself at a small writing desk and asked O'Brien his full name, the first full sentence which he had addressed to his charge. O'Brien answered, although he was unable to help on the spelling: Thomas Patrick O'Brien. Rory filled out the prepared declaration which would be appended to the documents drawn up by the solicitor. Then Rory prepared himself for the culmination of years of questing research.

The particulars of the ceremony shall not be recounted here; my time is a finite resource, and the newspapers have speculated and gloated over the dark deeds enacted in that chamber with varying levels of accuracy but with no insight into its true purpose. Suffice it to say that candles were lit and dark beings were supplicated in languages not heard ever before in civilized countries, and scarcely in the benighted corners of the globe in the last four thousand years. Rory nearly exhausted his weak frame in the execution of the rites which he had purposed, and in fact it was only the awareness that faltering in their performance after a certain point was warned to bring the blackest retribution of unrestrained occult powers which enabled him to continue after he had stretched his meager endurance beyond any exertion he had undertaken in his anemic life.

At the culmination of the rites, which the manacled but otherwise unrestrained O'Brien had endured with a resigned bemusement and appreciation for novelty giving way slowly to dull forebodings of doom, a darkness filled the room like a smoke, almost obscuring the candles lit at the cardinal compass points around the mystic circle. Rory felt a tingling in all of his skin as if a lightning strike was incipient. He opened his mouth to shout out the final syllables of the incantation which he had laborious transliterated into Roman characters for recitation, and as the words were formed they were torn from his mouth by an almost magnetic power inhabiting the clouded air of the room. Then the candles all went out at once, O'Brien screamed, and Rory knew no more.

The period of unconsciousness is yet nebulous, as Rory made no true return to consciousness for several hours, despite the vivid flashes of sensation punctuating the dreamlike maelstrom that was his only awareness until he came to himself in unexpected surroundings: a cell. It was not the same cell in which he had found O'Brien, but it was of a type—a temporary prison used by the police to hold miscreants until they were either released or remanded to the custody of the courts.

Rory stood and tried to see beyond the shadowed bars which demarcated his confinement. Then he started: he had stood, unassisted! He looked at his hands, and they weren't the reedlike bundle of scholar's fingers twisted by years of handling crutch or wheelchair; they were thick, meaty, calloused, and decorated with small cuts and scratches from which the dirt and blood had not been cleansed. He drew breath into a robust chest, filling his glorious frame with oxygen which energized his hale, energetic body. He, Rory, had accomplished his purpose: he was in O'Brien's body, having transmigrated according to the dark promises of manuscripts he had found hidden and unrecognized below the library.

His exultation, though, was short-lived, as his shouts of celebration had roused to his cell door the officer with charge of the prisoners. It was only through earnest supplication of this worthy that the events between the dark ceremony and Rory's return to awareness, and the reason for his present confinement, were explained to him, and Rory's spirits, which had reached a celestial height at confirmation of the accomplishment of his designs, were dashed to stygian darkness.

He understood now some of the inscrutable warnings from the books which he had glossed over in favor of more concrete instruction. Rory's soul, incarnated for so many years in a body which had had very little power of motion or energy, had suddenly found itself the master of an engine, as it were, of great abilities, of virility and passion, none of which he had ever learned to control as had O'Brien growing up with them. The transmigration had left him semi-insensate, and the instincts so long repressed in Rory's own spindly frame were suddenly given free reign in O'Brien's, untempered by any restrictive influence which his conscious mind would have provided. Unrestrained, the invalid in the athlete's body had rampaged from the estate and through the surroundings, hungering for the sensations and expressions which had so long been denied him, to a degree which he had not been aware even resided within his essence.

The policeman ended his account with a grim tally of his savage activities: three murders, two rapes, and countless severe injuries and injustices, all vouchsafed by multiple witness who had stood aghast at this feral man's appetite for perversion and destruction.

This, the list of concrete numbers which concluded the policeman's diatribe, sealed Rory's doom—or O'Brien's rather, for Rory had been conclusively identified as O'Brien by the police who finally cornered and restrained him, many of whom had had previous encounters with him in less extreme circumstances. And also laid to the blame of O'Brien was the death of the invalid Rory Calloran, whose lifeless body was found in the parlor from which O'Brien had burst by force, the victim of severe if as yet unexplained violence.

So now I sit awaiting the appointed hour of execution, when the robust and strong neck and spine of this hardy body will nevertheless meet its match in the hangman's craft. This writing will no doubt be deemed the ravings of a madman tinged by some instinct for confession; nevertheless, I here declaim and aver that though the thick, work-hardened fingers of Thomas O'Brien are those which hold this stub of pencil, it is the mind and soul of Rory Calloran which directs those fingers.

The Flooding of River Home

The homefathers and the exchangers avert their faces, and though they call me by my name WeSa to my face, behind my back when they think I cannot hear they call me "the Remnant of River Home." My wife, I hear, they call "Lament of the Unmothered." They do not shun us, of course, and most do not teach their own children to hate us, for no sin can be named to lay at my feet; I am incarnate the tragedy that befell River Home, but I am not its instigator, nor am I any more to blame than those swept away. The only one to revile me openly is my birthsister, forever named ErRu, and she shall have no children to teach her hatred to.

As grievous as this tragedy was, their whispered scorn would not be so great if I had not chosen as mate one who was already ill-omened in their eyes, she who was LuRa and had no birthbrother save the ungrown lump that was delivered with her. The tale passed down from the Forgotten Times is that those without a birthsibling were given to the River to avert bad fortune, but it is only a tale, and none can say if it was ever true. Still, the shadow of such legends lay heavy over her in her childhood, when she was LuRa and I was ErWe. And when I chose her to mate and to rename her WeRa to my WeSa—her, above all the pleading young women whose birth-brothers had been hale and hearty—then the whispers about her began anew on some lips, this time suggesting that the tragedy had been because of her after all, and by mating her I had invited the doom to linger and strike again, like a dark cloud wedged into the valley that brings no rain but only dry wind and lightning. But people say many things in anger and grief, to vent the ashes in their hearts.

When my first Longyear came, I was still an infant, clinging to my mother's fur alongside ErRu. I must have seen the young men enter the River to ride out the Flooding, but no memory of it had stayed with me until my own Longyear. I was not the youngest of the young men in that spring awaiting the Flooding, but my father privately fretted of my chances for taking a mate. "He's a small boy," he said when he and my mother thought I was outside. "Thin, too. The water'll wash him clean out of the valley, all the way down to the sea."

"He'll manage," my mother said. "The River is merciful, and capricious. You were no hulking brute yourself, remember."

"No, but I was older than ErWe," he said. "And I was certainly enough man for you, wasn't I?"

"You were, and are," she said, warming to his hand on her shoulder. And their conversation quickly moved on to other matters.

At least in the spring of Longyear, there was little anxiety about my prospects once out of the Flooding. It is said that one season, several Longyears ago, fevers had raged through the children of River Home, and unhappily taken more daughters than sons. There were simply not enough eager young women waiting on the shores when the newly-manned youths, bedraggled and gasping, hauled themselves from the floodwaters to claim their new names and new mates. Those who had been too slow, too beaten by the ordeal, had sloughed onto shore to find that only the pitying eyes of their parents and the oldsters were watching them, for the laughing girls had already run off with their dripping mudsodden husbands.

This Longyear, the lamentations would be taken up by at most two or three unmothered girls instead of unmated boys, for by health and happenstance the boys and girls who awaited the Flooding eagerly were almost perfectly matched, though there can always be some few young men whose grip and fortitude fail them in the rush of the waters. These things are taught to us: the frailest of the boys never emerge from the river, and the uncomeliest of the girls are never taken to mate, and thus the people are healthy, happy and beautiful in the River's mercy.

And also, tipping the balance even further, there was LuRa. It was casual talk around River Home that LuRa was of course destined to be one of the unmothered, because of the shadow of misfortune around her; some even quietly speculated whether she should not hide herself from the Flooding altogether, lest her presence at the River's bank bring woe. I let such voices chatter above and around me, and said nothing to gainsay them. But it was my purpose to take LuRa to mate, even then.

The vague mutterings of doom around her had never made sense to me in my infancy. To me then, she was simply a girl of my age, without a birthbrother who would push me around as the other, larger children did. We were friends before we went from four legs to two, and to most we were still merely friends, as children will be.

But LuRa and I knew differently. Her body had rounded and swollen in those places that should be ample in a woman, and the hair on my head had begun to crest. We shared time alone with each other, thinking not as children but with desire and anticipation pounding red behind our eyes. We spoke of it to none, but we looked forward to the Flooding as anxiously as any two other youths in River Home.

The eldest of the homefathers, XiHe, had sent his grown son JaZa to be the Far Trumpeter the day before the calendar predicted the Flooding. His leavetaking marked the beginning of the whole

Flooding ordeal and celebration for us, the young, who stood on either side of his path as he took the southward road on the east bank of the River, past the low cliffs near to River Home through which the River had cut a channel into the valley, using his worn map to find his way through the high cliffs a day's journey up the River's body. The young women dropped flowers after his passing where his feet had trod, an acknowledgment that by the time he returned on that same path, spring would truly have arrived in River Home. We young men stood on the opposite side of the path from the young women, shielding our eyes from the sun and almost trembling with anticipation.

All were at the muddy edge of the River at first full light the next morning, the excitement of the parents eclipsed by the anxious energy of the young. The parents and small children stopped high on the crest of the bank, well above the edge of the muddy wash that the Flooding of the last Longyear had deposited, the renewed soil that fairly seized the seeds we planted and threw forth crops in abundance. This had been a prosperous Longyear, the adults all said; for after the Flooding, the mud had stayed moist for months, and even after that there came gentle rains which watered the plants without washing the mud back into the River's flow. Good food and good water meant good living, and there were more children playing at the high water mark of the wash who had been born since the last Longyear than the oldsters ever remembered seeing.

The young women came down onto the banks that had been mudded and then planted so many times. Old XiLi, XiHe's mate, stopped them halfway up from the River, and they dispersed themselves, each finding a spot of clear earth in which they could sit and recline, each in full view of all of us young men who stood at the very edge of the water and rocks. XiHe was with us, solemnly instructing us, but each young man's ears were stoppered to XiHe's admonitions as our eyes sought out those to whom we most wanted to run, dripping and gasping, after the Flooding. I found LuRa and tried not to display my teeth in a smile of foolish eagerness. XiHe stood patiently as our attention was drawn elsewhere; he had seen six of these Longyears, and maybe even remembered the time when he himself had waded out into the River. He patiently used his stick to knock some shins, and our attention went back to him, though we could all feel the eyes of the expectant young women still upon us like a breeze on the fur on the backs of our legs.

"Let us pray," he said, and he bowed his head and stared down into the water up to his shins, the crest of his hair a bristly white stripe down his head and back. We all stepped into the cool River, feeling the tingle as the cold met the soles of our feet, and each stared down into the clear water that flowed, unhurried but constant, around our legs and on down the river. XiHe prayed in words that had long fallen away from the everyday tongues of the people; his cadence was that of one who learns the sounds at the feet of another, whose mouth makes its forms from obeisance rather than intent. These, I knew, were words handed down from eldest of the old to eldest of the old from so far back in time that the River alone matched them for age. The people of River Home birth and age and marry and die; the River runs on, and the prayers to and for it linger just that long, passing to new sets of lips as the old ones go silent.

The prayer ended and XiHe raised his head. We all did likewise, blinking in the sun, and I think we all involuntarily looked to the shore for an instant, reassuring ourselves that the young eager women were still there. I moved my weight from foot to foot as each slid into the silt that lined the edge of the River.

We stood in silence, listening to the murmur of the River, the whine of insects which flitted over River and shore and alighted harmlessly on fur. We watched XiHe, who steadied himself with his staff in the gentle current. His eyes were closed; he was listening. As were we all.

And together we heard it, distant but unmistakable even to those of us who couldn't remember it from the last Longyear: the high-pitched braying of the Far Trumpeter perched on the cliffs that marked the horizon to the south. XiHe's son JaZa could see the Flood coming.

XiHe opened his eyes as the crackle of excitement passed over all those in the River and on the land. "You who are to brave the River this Longyear," he addressed us, and his voice cracked to reach all of us over the steady babble of the River, "find the spots in which you will withstand the embrace of the River. Some of you, the River may take to herself, and all of us in River Home salute you now, for we will not have occasion later. Those whom the River leaves will then find the embrace of your mates, and we will have ample time to salute you afterward. Go now."

And we turned as one from XiHe and looked to the River.

The rocks which punctuated the River here were washed down from the distant cliffs, it is said, and stuck out from the flowing water here and there, in ones and twos and threes. Some had been smoothed where the water flows eternally past them, but most had spent the endless years sticking out above the waterline, and remained rough-edged and craggy. Birds perched on a few, and white streaks from their droppings striped the tallest ones. These few stones were our safety. To the south, at the closer end of the valley, the River flowed eternally through the breach in the low cliffs; north of this garden of stones, the River swept unbroken until it exited the valley far to the north.

I was small and spry. I dashed out into the current with leaping steps to keep from having to drag my legs through the water, very conscious that such bounding was boyish, not manly. But it didn't matter much. Emerging from the River after the Flooding would confer and prove manhood more than my gait. My object was a small cluster of three stones, the one in the middle taller than the rest and leaning forward into the current. I knew that wrapping my arms around that taller stone, with the two on the sides to shield me, would offer me as much protection as could be had in the Flooding.

Others also headed toward that same trio of stones, but I got there first; grumbling, they turned aside to grasp other rocky anchors. The River here didn't lack for such stones; this was why the Flooding was always observed at this spot.

XiHe stayed in the River up to his knees, leaning on his short staff, until all the young males had chosen an anchor. Then we all heard it from the distant cliffs: the second warning blast from the Far Trumpeter. XiHe nodded, raised a hand in mute benediction, and turned his silvered mane to the shore where his XiLi waited for him with a staff of her own; together they helped each other up the sloping bank.

My eyes turned from their old hobbling shapes further up the River's bank, seeking out my LuRa. All of the young eager females had now moved back to the crest of the bank, and their silhouettes against the sky as they stood or crouched were almost indistinguishable one from another.

It was because my attention was focused on the land that I didn't notice SuChi nearing me until his heavy hand fell on my shoulder and pulled. "My spot, ErWe," he said gruffly, and with a single tug yanked me clear from the trio of stones that had been my sure protection. SuChi was the heaviest of the young males in the River; he had matured quickly, and was half again as heavy as I was. The defiant sound in my throat died without passing my lips; there was no way that I could defend my spot, no way in which I could pry SuChi's strong, fleshy arms from the tallest of the three stones and reclaim my place.

I looked desperately to the shore. XiHe's back was still turned as he and his wife clambered up the slope, and I knew that SuChi had used what passed for cleverness in his brain, waiting until the old silvermane's gaze was no longer enforcing custom and order.

And then, as I stood waist-deep in the cold rushing water, I heard the sound of the third trumpet. The Flooding was near; even had XiHe still been turned toward the River, there was no time to plead my case and regain my rightful spot. Nothing stops the Flooding.

There were still vacant stones, I could see, but they were too far for me to get to now that the third trumpet had sounded. All of the most viable nearby stones had been taken by those my age who now watched me as I cast this way and that, seeking refuge like a mouse cut off from its hole.

At last I dashed forward into the current, past the spot where SuChi crouched in safety and smirked. There was another stone a dozen paces beyond it, unoccupied and standing slightly out of the water. Its sides were slick and smooth, and it tilted back, danger-ously so. But the third trumpet had sounded, and the Flooding would not wait. I splashed forward and wrapped my arms around it, locking my wrists awkwardly as the trumpet sounded again.

Again? It took half a heartbeat to realize it. The warning trum-pet sounds three times, no more; everyone knows that. But it had sounded a fourth time. And now, a fifth. Even above the murmur of the River, I imagined I could hear the muted voices of consterna-tion on the shore. I glanced over and saw XiHe and others shield-ing their eyes to look in vain toward the far cliffs where JaZa now blew ragged blasts on the horn one after another with scarcely a breath in between.

I craned my neck around my stone and looked forward to the gap in the low cliffs through which the River pours into the basin of River Home. It loomed too close for any of us in the River to even pretend to see where JaZa was perched on the high cliffs be-yond. I could only see the channel in the rocky walls cut and deep-ened by the eternal River, its walls stained above the current water level with the marks of the high water of Floodings past. A roar started out of that gap, a heaving of rough wind as the Flooding drove the air before it.

And then I saw it. And I forgot to breathe.

The Flooding was coming. It was a wall of water thick with the silt and mud of the spring runoff, churning with the violence of its approach. And it was twice as high as the highest mark on the wall of the gap.

JaZa still blew his horn, but it faded behind the steady exhaled roar of the oncoming water, a Flooding unlike any ever seen before. I only just remembered myself and gasped a full breath before the Flooding hit.

The water was a solid thing of cold and fury, as hard and crushing as the stone around which my arms were desperately wrapped. It hit my face and front as hard as if I had been standing unprotected in mid-River, and pulled my back like a thousand SuChis with their fingers entwined into my fur. The water beat at my hands clasped together around the stone; the cold and pressure ground them like millstones until my fingers were left insensate. I could feel bubbling panic forcing its way into my lungs, pushing up through my mouth and nostrils. This Flooding wasn't the River rising up to claim the weak as her own mates; she was a raging animal, the queen of demons, lashing out with her pent-up fury at poor little ErWe who had dared into her unstoppable, murderous path.

I only knew that my numb fingers had let go when I felt the water carry me backwards instead of pushing against me. I gave myself up for lost and hoped that the River would deposit me in the next world before my lungs burst.

Then something struck me in the back—or rather, I struck it. I had to clap both hands to my mouth to keep the stale air in my lungs from jetting out in surprise and pain. The small of my back was against a stone in the River, the very same stone, I realized, where I had confidently positioned myself before SuChi dragged me from my place. The forward stone angled down into the current, and it was there that the current held me, pinned by the water at the angle where the leaning stone met the River bottom. The Flooding bent my head back and tore at my eyes and nostrils, but my back was securely wedged under the stone.

I crawled one hand up the surface of the stone that held me, hoping to find the air above the churning water; but if I reached it, my senseless fingers could not tell the difference between wet and dry. The other hand I balled into a fist and pressed against my stomach, willing myself to hold the desperate breath that hammered on the inside of my chest to be let out. All of us had practiced holding our breath, together and separately, in the open and with our faces in basins of cold water, but who could have imagined the fury that the River would unleash upon the eager young men of River Home?

Then, when my lungs were fighting for fresh air like a trapped beast, when I was nearly ready to breathe the water in just to end the oppressive anxious need, I felt the River's pressure slacken. Not much, but enough that my head wasn't bent almost backwards with the current. I stretched both hands toward the rock face and turned myself to face the stone which had held me down and kept me from being swept away. My fingers were no better than broken sticks, but I clumsily pulled myself upright against the current—still strong enough to whisk me away like a dried leaf, but compared to what it had been it felt like the sloshings in a washtub—and finally, finally, my face broke through the frothing surface. I released the breath I had held for what seemed like a full Longyear and gasped in new air that burned all the way down my throat unto lungs that could not wait to expel this breath and draw in the next and the next and the next.

My eyes felt bruised when I opened them. They probably were, having faced the River water which had struck me like fists. I looked around for SuChi in fear that he would peel me from "his" stone and I would be swept away after all, down the River and out of the valley. But I could not see SuChi through my blurry eyes.

I clung to the stone and gasped, feeling my blood brighten and my head clear. The overlapping aches of my body, overshadowed until now by the all-encompassing pummeling of the River, began to fight each other for my attention, and I knew that by tomorrow I would be a single massive bruise under my fur, barely able to move.

But tomorrow I would be alive. And LuRa would be there to

tend me, LuRa who I would now rename WeRa as soon as I reached shore and discarded the name my parents had given me, ErWe, and named myself WeSa as an adult.

I brushed the fur around my eyes with one hand to clear the mud and blinked toward shore, ill-focused like a newborn. I could see the father and mothers, the oldsters, and the waiting young women at the top of the shore. I could see the line of churned wash along the slope of the shore, higher than I had ever known it could reach. The roaring within my ears dimmed, and beyond the continued slosh and rush of the River, there was no other sound.

Finally I judged and hoped that the current of the Flooding was weak enough and my own feet strong enough to let go of my stone and make my way to shore. I set one foot solidly on the bottom, then the other, leaning sideways into the current. I took another step. And another.

Then I looked for SuChi again, realizing what it meant that he was not clinging to the same stone I had been. He was gone? Had the Flooding truly swept away the strongest of the youths of this Longyear? I could not see him, and though I had been torn from my own mooring and yet lived, such a happenstance was not to be trusted twice; I had never heard of it happening before, in all the tales told of Longyears past. SuChi was a bully and a braggart, exulting in his size and his early cresting as if it were a thing earned and merited, but even so his loss was the first I had ever known. He was my age, and now he was dead.

Then I looked to the other stones and groups of stones, sticking from the River with the dirty wash of the Flooding curled around them.

I saw no one else.

I stood there, dumb, staring from rock to rock as the truth of it sank slowly into my soggy mind. Save for the stones which had stood there for Longyears out of memory, I was alone in the River.

My eyes followed the current downstream. Past this field of stones, where the youths of every Longyear clung to show their fitness to be men, the path of the River was unbroken again until it finally passed out of sight at the north end of the valley of River Home. There were no outcroppings to provide purchase for desperate fingers, no curls where eddies might drag the fortunate out of the current and toward the bank; all who lost their grip during the Flooding were taken far out of the valley, and if their bodies were ever brought to shore again in a distant land before the River reached the sea, none knew it.

I could feel all eyes upon me from the bank. I stumbled as I waded through the water still as high as my chest, feeling the weight of attention. I could feel the grit and silt that had saturated my fur. I tried to concentrate only on my footing, but while I did not look up at the score of stunned, devastated females on land, I could hear them: a nasal keening from the back of their throats that rose unbidden in desperation, both mournful and pleading.

When I reached the shallows where the water was below my knees—and I realized how much further up the bank this point still was than when I had entered the water surrounded by young hopefuls—I could no longer maintain the pretense of deliberation over my footing and looked up. There, the young women who had had their own favorites swept away watched me, eyes bright with a desperate hope. Almost all of them had slipped down the slope toward me, as if I might simply choose the one who was closest to be my mate. Some reached a hand out to me in supplication. Some even threw aside shame and stretched their legs wide to offer me the moistness peeking from their fur, as if a mere glimpse could entice me. I passed these brazen ones, who suddenly closed themselves as if awakening to their shame.

I could choose any of them. It was a realization that sat on the surface of my stunned mind, a fact which seemed to have no personal import to me, like something memorized in schooling. It meant nothing to me. I had already made my choice.

I stepped out of the eddying water onto the dry earth. Slowly, wearily, I walked up the slope. I looked neither to left nor right, and the keening rose full-throated in every young woman I passed, consigned by my passage to fruitless spinsterhood. I saw the parents and oldsters who had prepared of a day of uncertain celebration, now watching me in silent grief. My own mother and father were somewhere in the crowd; they had been rooted to their spots in shock, and I could not see them as I ascended further and further the shallow slope of the River's bank.

But I was not looking for them. I had eyes only for LuRa, who still sat on the summit of the bank, legs folded demurely under her, eyes averted in either excitement or sorrow or both.

I leaned over when I reached her, almost falling to my knees in stiff weariness, and kissed her.

And the keening behind me became a full-throated wail, drowning out whatever we might have said after that.

The only one who openly hates me is my birthsister ErRu, who lives still with my parents and will help raise their coming birthpair. While all of the other females had still held out a slim hope that they would yet mate, when she saw me stand alone from the embrace of the River she knew there was not even that hope for her; for what could she do, when the only eligible male to emerge from the Flooding was her birthbrother? The other young women lamented that their chosen had not come back out of the River; ErRu hated that I had.

But hatred and mourning and lamentation notwithstanding, LuRa and I were married by that kiss. I took the name WeSa and renamed her WeRa, and together we built our thatched home on the edge of River Home. We had no lack of building supplies; quiet and sad-eyed parents brought what they had saved for their own sons and daughters and left it silently at the site we had chosen. We used what was needful and returned the rest to the gathering place in the center of River Home. We did not want to build a spacious home on the backs of so many grieving families.

Already XiHe and the oldsters have circulated through River

Home, gently encouraging all who are still able to have more child-ren so that there will not be a bare generation in years to come. Already the bellies begin to swell, the breasts to hang. WeRa joins them in their fecundity, and I delight in feeling the firm tautness of her belly and imagine that I can feel the two little bodies inside, still too small and weak to kick at the pressure of my palm.

I hope it is two bodies. If one of our first birthing were to come stillborn, the whispers which still circulate about WeRa—given re-newed voice by the injury and the covetousness of what happened in the River—would no longer be spoken without voice, but would be shouted on the footpaths and in the doorways: that she is ill-omened and her child without a birthsibling perpetuates a curse on River Home. There would even be talk of returning to the old ways of the Bad Times, when those born alone are given to the River. No one has said such things to me, but I know them to be true nonetheless. The mouth is not the only member that speaks, and the ear not the only one that hears.

So we hope for a healthy pair, and we go about our business, avoiding the shadows that lurk behind every conversation. Another Longyear will come, and whether the Flooding is as it was in times past or whether it chooses to rage again, they cannot blame my WeRa or me for it this time. We will do what we can, and bear as many fine strong children as come to us, and we will go on with our lives, thanking the River for mercy shown.

Other Duties

Note: This story was written specifically for the *Monsters & Mormons* anthology, which deals—as the title suggests—with monsters and Mormons. As such, it's replete with LDS in-jokes. I apologize if non-Mormons don't get them. Trust me, they're funny.

The voice on the other end of the telephone line overflowed with nervousness and apology. "Hi— Bishop Evenson? This is, my name is Steve Roundy, from the West Point Fourteenth Ward. I'm really sorry to bother you so late, but I heard that you're the agent bishop for stuff like this..."

"I am." Norman Evenson rubbed the gummy stuff from the inside corners of his eyes with the thumb and forefinger of his other hand. He could see his wife Miriam up on one elbow, watching him. Beyond her, the digital clock read "1:32 AM" in glowing green. He gestured to her to go back to sleep and stood up, taking the phone with him as he walked out of the bedroom toward his home office.

"Tell me what the problem is," Norman said as he flipped on the light and squinted.

❖

It took a little over ten minutes for Norman to get from Brother Roundy the salient details. After he hung up, he put on the white shirt, tie and Dockers that he kept in his office so he could get dressed at odd hours without waking Miriam. He avoided his two-piece suits for matters like this; not only were they all dry-clean only, but their crotches tended to split out if things got active. When the tie was knotted, he called his first counselor, Brant DeSalle.

"Sorry to wake you, Brant," Norman said, the phone cradled in his neck as he slipped on his shoes. "We've got a call to handle."

"Oh. Mercy." Norman could hear the lag as Brant's sleepy brain caught up to his words. "I don't need to shave, do I?"

"I'm not going to. Give Brother Wills a call and have him meet us... Wait, he's still out of town, isn't he?"

"Baby blessing up in Idaho, back Thursday," Brant said.

"Right. Don't worry about it, then. I'll see you at the church in fifteen minutes."

After he hung up and tied his shoes, Norman flipped back through his stake calendar. It was the first week of February; he had only been the agent bishop since the start of the year, and this was only their third real call. Maybe he could call the previous agent bishop to put together the needed quorum.

There was no answer at Bishop Stewart's home number, so he called his cellphone. It took three rings for him to pick up.

"Bishop Stewart, this is Bishop Evenson. Sorry to call at this hour, but we got an emergency call and my second counselor is out of town. I wonder if you can help us out."

"Yeah, I'm in Barbados on a cruise ship," said Bishop Stewart.

"Oh. Sorry to bother you, then."

"Best of luck, though."

Norman ended the call and paged again through the directory. The next person in the ward who held priesthood keys was Kyle McMullin, who had come back from his mission in May, gotten married in November, and been called as the elders quorum president in December. Norman doubted that the high councilor had even given Kyle's presidency any training yet on the full scope of the agent ward's duties. But that was the way the line of authority ran.

He dialed Kyle's number. "G'day," said a groggy voice. Norman smiled. Sometimes when caught off guard, Kyle slipped back into the accent he had picked up on his mission in Australia.

"President McMullin, this is the Bishop. Sorry to wake you, but I need your help."

Norman got to the bishop's office before Brother DeSalle or President McMullin. He had time to kneel and pray in silence; then he unlocked his desk and reached past the calling forms and welfare carbons in their hanging folders to the locked box at the bottom of the drawer. He had just set it on the top of his desk when Brother DeSalle entered, followed by the elders quorum president, who was still tying his tie.

"Thank you, brethren," Norman said. "I hope we can get this handled quickly." He looked at Kyle's sleepy, confused face. "President McMullin, I think I need to explain a few things to you…"

Norman was right; Kyle hadn't been trained on any of this, and sat stunned as Norman sketched in their extra duties.

"So…" Kyle said, trying to use his missionary *restate* skills to wrap his mind around the situation. "…You're the agent bishop for supernatural stuff?"

Norman nodded. "'Paranormal and Occult.' Just since January. It's an annual rotation through the local stakes in northern Davis County. That makes our entire ward the agent ward, so in Brother Wills's absence, the duty falls to you."

"Wow." Kyle swallowed. "Should I have, like, brought my consecrated oil?"

"We have plenty." Norman inserted a key from his ring of church keys into the lock on the front of the box. "And some other things."

In the velvet-lined tray inside was a set of three gold-colored medallions on leather thongs. Norman took them out and handed one each to DeSalle and Kyle. DeSalle slipped his on over his head; Kyle watched him and followed suit. Norman put on his own and then removed from the same tray three spritzer bottles with short straps attached. He passed them around.

"As much oil as you'll need."

DeSalle leaned over to Kyle. "When you need to use it, put the strap around your wrist. Oil on your hands gets slippery. You don't want that. Trust me, I know."

"You guys have done this before?" Kyle asked.

"Yes, but don't ask us about it," Norman said. "It's confidential, just like a disciplinary council."

Norman pulled out the velvet-lined tray. Beneath it was another tray, this one containing a long-barreled six-shooter of burnished silvery steel, with cream-colored porcelain grips and accents. Kyle gaped at the gun but said nothing.

A small wooden box also nestled in the tray contained cartridges, and Norman began loading the gun. The bullets weren't metallic; they looked like clay, and on each there were inscribed tiny symbols. To Norman they looked like the "Book of Mormon Egyptian" characters on the souvenir bricks one bought in Nauvoo, but he was no expert; they could have been old-world Egyptian, or Hebrew, or even Adamic for all he knew.

"We forgot to replenish our supply of these after our last time out," Norman said. "Remind me to have one of the clerks order some more on Sunday."

"Will do," DeSalle said.

Norman snapped the revolver's cylinder shut. "Well, brethren," he said, "I think a prayer is in order." He lowered himself to his knees, and the other two men did likewise.

They took Norman's Kia and drove in silence. The suburban regularity of Clinton faltered as they drove west, with clumped developments alternating with horse pastures and hay fields. The last snowfall had been a week before, but cold daytime temperatures had kept it powdery, and in spots it had drifted in half-hearted streaks across the blacktop.

A couple of miles after they passed the last streetlight, DeSalle in the passenger seat checked a reflective street sign on their right against the sticky note that Norman had given him. "Turn here," he said, "and then the second left, first house on the right."

Norman turned just after a sign that read, "CASTLEVIEW MEADOWS PHASE I COMING SOON—RESERVE YOUR LOT NOW!" Following DeSalle's directions, he pulled in by a thirty-year-old split-level that had been built on a large country lot. The night sky was punctuated with clouds, and once the headlights were off Norman could see a long backyard separating the house from a horse barn, and fence-posts beyond that marking a horse pasture.

They stepped out of the Kia in their parkas; Kyle also wore a cap with flaps down over his ears. As they started trudging toward the house, the front door popped open and out came a man with a camo hunting jacket thrown on over a sweatshirt and sweatpants.

"Oh, thank God!" he said. "I mean—I'm Steve Roundy. Bishop...?"

Norman waved to show which one he was. "I'm Bishop Evenson. When did this all start, again?"

Steve stuck his bare hands in his pocket. His tennis shoes were untied, and his feet shifted in the cold.

"Last night, I guess. I mean, Amy said there was something wrong—that's my daughter—she said for a couple of weeks that something was wrong, but, you know..."

"Is your daughter here?"

"No. My wife took both kids into Ogden to her mother's house, right about when I called you."

Norman nodded. "So what have you seen?"

"Well, what I heard first was the horses... Do you want to come inside?"

Kyle started moving toward the house, but Norman shook his head. "We ought to go right to work."

"Right." Steve led the way around the house, and they trudged in single file toward the horse barn. "Well, as I said on the phone, we heard something, Amy and I, we heard something from the barn last night. The horses were noisy, whinnying and dancing around. We went out after dinner, and we couldn't see anything wrong, so we just left them to settle down on their own. But they kept getting noisier. Finally, around midnight, we were worried and couldn't sleep, so I went out again. The horses were screaming by this point like there was a rattler in their stalls or something, so I went in, and before I reached the light switch I saw..."

Steve stopped, and the other three stopped behind him. They were in the backyard now, closer to the barn than the house on a well-worn path through the snow.

"...Eyes. I saw eyes, red and glowing. Like in the movies. I've never seen things like that for real, though. It wasn't like cat's eyes reflecting—these were glowing like hot coals. And a voice... I don't know what it said, but it rumbled so low I could feel it in the soles of my feet, inside my boots. That's when I ran back to the house, Nicole bundled up the kids, and I called the bishop, and he gave me your number."

Norman looked at the barn, sturdy and unpainted. There were two glass windows on this side; nothing showed through them but darkness.

"Is that a new development going in over there, Brother Roundy?"

It took Steve a second to catch up to the change of subject. "Uh, yeah. They broke ground and started laying out lots in the fall. Used to be an alfalfa field. Why?"

Instead of answering the question, Norman asked, "How many horses do you have?"

"Two," Steve said. "Chaser and Star."

"They're quiet now."

"I know. They got quiet sometime after I got inside. After I called you, I stuck my head out to hear, and I couldn't hear anything."

Norman nodded.

"Well, let's get this started."

He raised his arm to the square."

"By the power of the Holy Melchi—"

He broke off as one barn window shattered, and something sailed out, whirling end over end. Norman leaped to the side; it landed roughly where he had been. It was a horse's head, white with a black patch between the wide-open eyes. The steaming neck was severed messily, like it had been taken off with a chainsaw. Norman felt wet spots on his pants and looked down. Blood from the neck had splattered up his pant leg as it flew through the air. The hot blood immediately turned cold.

Behind him, Kyle breathed, "Oh, man..."

Steve swallowed. "That's Star," he said. His voice sounded like he was trying to hold back a sneeze.

Norman unzipped his parka to give him clear access to the gun in his belt. "Brother Roundy, once we go in the door, where is the light switch?"

Steve was still staring at the horse's head on the snow. "To your left, when you go in. On the stud, about three feet in."

Norman looked back over his shoulder. DeSalle watched him, his lips together in a thin line. Kyle's eyes kept returning to the horse's head, but he didn't seem to be hyperventilating or trembling.

"Brother Roundy, you stay here and listen for us." He nodded to the other two. "Let's go."

They approached the barn quietly, but didn't bother trying to be sneaky; whatever was inside obviously knew they were here. A couple of times Norman thought he heard breaths or snorts. The other horse? It could still be alive; the head that was thrown out at them had obviously been alive recently enough for the blood to be fresh.

"Oil out," he murmured to the other two.

He heard DeSalle tell Kyle, "Put it in your left hand so you can raise your right arm to the square."

"Oh. Got it."

At the barn's double doors they stopped. Norman's nose had begun to run, and he wiped it quickly on the back of his sleeve. He noticed that Kyle had put his earflaps up.

Norman waved DeSalle to the left side of the double door. "Okay," he said. "One, two..."

On "three," DeSalle yanked the door open, and Norman jumped inside, fumbling for the light switch. He heard a snuffling sound, and then drowning it out a deep rumble, like an asthmatic whale. Then the bare lights bulbs came on.

At the far end of the barn, beside the horse stalls, was a monstrous humanoid figure, probably topping ten feet. At first glance, it was an articulated human skeleton. At second glance it wasn't terribly human, even allowing for the size; swept-back spines grew out of its skull and down its back, and the orbital sockets in its face were drawn triangular into a scowl instead of showing the round-eyed surprise of a human skull. On third glance, it was more than just a skeleton; its bones were held together by a thin layer of red meat and glistening tendons, as if it had been recently and deeply flayed. Norman saw, on the floor behind it, a pile of moist, bloody bones, and understood: the skeleton hadn't recently lost flesh, it had recently gained it from the slaughtered horse.

Where was the other horse? The stall doors were open. One was empty; the other—yes, the horse was on its side on the straw, shuddering. Did horses faint? This one might have.

The skeletal thing watched Norman with its eyeless eyes, a glottal clicking or purring coming from its throat. Norman had seen the movie *Predator* once on TV; it sounded like that.

"Brethren," he whispered loudly, and DeSalle and Kyle edged into the barn, their eyes on the skeleton. Even without eyes in its sockets, Norman could sense its attention focusing on each of them in turn.

It spoke. Its voice vibrated like a passing freight train; the consonants were thick and grating. Norman couldn't understand the words, but he felt the menace in them. They were being warned.

"Okay," he said to the others, keeping his voice to a whisper. It probably couldn't understand them any better than they could understand it, but he didn't want to spur it to action. "We're going to try to corner it in the empty stall where I can get a good shot at it. Oil ready? Go!"

The three men spread out, advancing at the skeleton with their spray bottles held up. Norman could sense surprise from the thing as he spritzed out a fine mist of consecrated oil in its direction, surprise that turned into malice. It started backing up as the three advanced. Then it whirled and leaped into the stall, and from there it climbed up the wall, its long partially-fleshed limbs sure and spidery. Norman hadn't been expecting that.

It easily reached the top of the barn's space, where beams and girders held up the peaked roof in shadows that the light bulbs barely reached. They craned their necks to keep it in sight as it clambered as fast as a man can run, and Norman could tell it was bearing down on him specifically; it had identified him as the leader. It leaned down suddenly and raked a clawed hand at him, and Norman dove to the side to avoid the long fingers. He rolled over a hay bale awkwardly and landed hard on his left shoulder.

"Hey!" Kyle shouted, his voice breaking. He dashed forward and spritzed his oil on the still grasping arm. The thing shrieked like rusty metal being dragged across concrete and pulled back its limbs.

Kyle was still aiming his oil at the roof while DeSalle helped Norman to his feet. "Bishop?"

"I'm all right. Just clumsy."

The skeleton scrambled back and forth, glaring at them from its eyeless face, with an agility that Norman wouldn't have expected from a twelve-foot skeleton crawling through the crosspieces of a barn roof. There was no way he could get a clear shot at it. He glanced behind them; the barn door stood a few feet open as they had left it.

"Kyle," he said, "go close the door."

"Maybe we ought to call the hotline," said DeSalle.

"You know Salt Lake won't get any specialists here before dawn," Norman said. "Now that we've got it angry, who knows how much damage it'd do before then?"

Kyle got the door closed, and he sprayed the handles with oil for good measure. The thing growled.

"All right, I have a plan," Norman said. "You two go back by the door."

DeSalle walked backwards to where Kyle was already standing. Norman side-walked to the opposite end of the barn, by the stalls. The thing above them hissed and scratched at the beams.

Norman carefully stowed his bottle of oil in his pocket. Then he grasped the medallion around his neck and pulled it off over his head. He held it a moment so its golden glint could catch the light, then tossed it in the straw on the floor, only a few feet in front of him.

"Bishop!" shouted DeSalle. "What are you doing?!"

The skeletal thing watched Norman intently. Then, as if drawn by an urge it couldn't control, it started down from the roof like a spider examining something caught in its web.

Norman stood empty-handed with his arms well away from his body, feeling like a gunfighter in an old Western. There was a na-ked place around his neck where the medallion should be.

Closer, just a little closer...

The thing paused, clinging to the wall and looking down at Nor-man. Then with a burst of speed it dropped to the floor in a crouch and launched itself in his direction on all fours.

"Arms to the square!" Norman yelled. He did so himself, draw-ing the gun from his belt with his left hand. His left shoulder ached where it had hit the floor, but the thing was close enough that his bad aim wouldn't matter.

"By the power of—" he started as he pulled the trigger. The rest of his words were lost in a sound like a pressurized airplane cabin being breached. There was no recoil from the gun; as far as Norman could tell, the clay bullets always vaporized into dust instead of going anywhere. But the thing shrieked and recoiled like it had been hit by a cannonball. It fell backwards, folding at odd angles, and Norman could see its stolen flesh start to curl off it before it even hit the floor. The bones that hit the floor were lifeless and inert.

He motioned to DeSalle and Kyle to come close and they did so, their oil held at the ready. Norman nudged the skull with his boot; it was now just a pile of gargantuan bones, surrounded by slivers of meat that sloughed off it and soaked the straw.

"It's a Gadianton," he said. "Brigham Young said that the Wasatch Front was thick with their spirits. I'm guessing that the heavy machinery for that subdivision disturbed it, and then once the winter solstice freed it, it started to wander."

"And the... meat?" said Kyle.

"Gadiantons are robbers, always have been," said DeSalle. "This one stole flesh to clothe itself." DeSalle looked up at Norman, comprehension settling in his eyes. "And you knew that a robber would go for the gold. That's why you took off your medallion—as bait."

"Actually," said Norman, "I think it saw I was unguarded and decided to come for me. One way or another, though, it worked."

"That... was... *cool!*" Kyle exclaimed. "It was so awesome! Chew on *that* Priesthood, you Son of Perdition!"

Norman looked at DeSalle. "I guess that's better than the reaction Brother Wills had the first time."

When they trudged back out of the barn, Steve was standing where they had left him on the path, his bare hands stuck under the arms of his coat for warmth, shifting from foot to foot.

"Is—did you—"

Norman nodded. "Taken care of. Your other horse is alive, but I don't know about injuries."

"Thank you. Thank you!" Steve grabbed Norman's hand and shook it ferociously.

"I can provide a letter for your insurance, but it'll have to be vague; it might not be helpful. Give me a call after you talk to your carrier."

"I will! I will—thank you!"

Norman turned to DeSalle and Kyle, who was grinning from ear to ear. "If I get you both the paperwork tomorrow night—or tonight, I guess—can you have it finished by Sunday? We're supposed to turn it in to the Presiding Bishopric's Office within a week."

DeSalle nodded. Kyle said, "Can do!"

"And cleanup?" DeSalle said.

"The PBO will want the bones, too," Norman said. "I know just the person."

He pulled out his phone and scrolled through to a stored number. After two rings, he said, "Sister Cotter, this is Bishop Evenson. I'm sorry to bother you so late, but you're the agent Relief Society president in these cases..."

Story in a Bar

Larry leaned toward the fellow sitting on the barstool two down. "So," he said, "how'd you lose the leg?"

The man swiveled slightly on his stool and looked at Larry, and Larry looked back. He knew he wasn't much to look at—Cindy had told him so for years, first jokingly, then simply as a matter of thoughtless habit—but he knew that he fit in, here in The Drowned Out, with the other low-grade white collar types who were taking up space at the bar and in the booths. He belonged. This one-legged man, though, was a novelty. His hair was white with a few scattered black threads running through it where it fell into his eyes; his skin was wrinkled leather as if he had spent fifty years staring down the wind and the sun, and his chin was frosted with white stubble. He wore a pea jacket, clinching Larry's assessment of the man as an "old salt," though what an "old salt" was doing in Ohio he had no idea. And of course there was that missing leg, without a prosthesis or even a peg in its place; the right leg of the man's corduroys were rolled and pinned where the thigh abruptly ended.

The man took a long pull at his beer as he looked back at Larry, then said, "You're a friendly sort, at you?" His muttered voice was strong but quiet, with a cadence that made Larry think of rolling seas and creaking yardarms or whatever creaked on a boat. Larry had never been on the ocean. He also knew that he was moderately drunk.

"Well, you seem like a man with a story," Larry said, waving to Chuck behind the bar for another of what he had just finished. "No point in ignoring it, right? The leg, I mean. Everyone's always try-ing to pretend that nobody's got a handicap—no offense—but hey, the leg's not there, and it's hard to ignore. And it's probably a damned interesting story."

"I'm sure everyone in here has his own story," the man said—not brusquely, not in an effort to end the exchange, but conversa-tional-like. Larry scooted his drink with him as he moved to the stool beside the man. Up close the old pea coat was patched but clean, and despite the stubble and shaggy hair, the man didn't smell or anything.

"Everyone in here," Larry said, "has the *same* story. Me too. Got a wife waiting at home who ain't really waiting. No matter when I get there, she'll be sitting up in bed with the mudpack on, watching whoever's on late-nite now, and when I crawl into bed she'll turn out the light and roll over and that'll be it. As long as I'm not getting any tonight, I might as well be here at The Drowned Out, getting pleasantly plastered. And there aren't any one-legged men at home. At least, I don't think her tastes run that way. So? What's your story?"

The man hadn't reacted as Larry slid over. He still didn't move, except for his eyes—or one eye, anyway. Larry guessed that the eye that didn't move was blind. The good eye flicked down to his empty beer and back. Larry waved to Chuck to give the man a refill. Chuck would just put it on his tab; Larry was a regular, and he liked the feel of that.

The man turned the handle of the fresh mug around to himself. "A story, then," he said. "Let me tell you a story. A story about a man named McCabe. McCabe was a sailor, first in the navy during the war, then on merchant ships afterward. Never wanted to settle down, this McCabe. He was fine with the wandering life, taking jobs as they came and leaving them when he felt like it.

"One trip, on his way across the Pacific—McCabe was the Mate on that run, on a small shipping vessel that ran among the Pacific Islands—the ship got blown off course during a storm, and when the sky cleared they were near a little cluster of islands that they would have missed if not for the storm. The captain wanted to take a day to check for leaks and tighten the bolts, so they moored close to one of the islands—a wee little thing, just big enough to walk around in an hour. The ship checked out fine, all except some work on the engine that you needed some expertise to handle, so only two or three men on board kept working, and McCabe was bored, so he took some fellows to explore the island."

Once he got started, Larry noticed, the man had a lilt to his voice, like he was one generation away from wherever his parents had been born. That kind of not-quite accent gave music to the telling of the tale, and Larry could almost smell the brine.

"So McCabe and his friends hopped to the island and started walking around it. They were almost completely on the other side when they saw what looked like old bricks on the beach. They were rounded by sand and surf, and deep green instead of red, but they were bricks. Now, the tide isn't going to wash something as heavy as bricks in from the ocean, especially not out in the middle of nowhere, so they must have come from someplace just off the beach. So McCabe and his friends went up the beach and into the trees to find out where the bricks came from."

The man shifted on his stool, and Larry saw his crutch for the first time, leaning against the bar on his other side. It was an adjustable crutch, modern and aluminum, but the original padding on the top had been replaced with some kind of hairy black and white pelt, like badger or skunk, sewn on with shoelaces.

"Not far under the trees, they found a building made of the same green bricks, no larger than a garden shed, with a low brick wall around it that was crumbling into the moss; that wall was where the bricks on the beach had come from. The building didn't have any windows, and it didn't really have a door, not anymore. They could tell where a doorway had originally been, but it had been filled in with the same bricks that made up the little building, all green stone which was now even greener with moss and lichen.

"McCabe hopped over the bit of wall, and he and his friends looked at the filled-up doorway. The little building still held together, four walls and a roof, but if there ever had been any mortar between the bricks in the doorway, it was all crumbled and washed out now, and when they tested the bricks at the top of the doorway, they found they were loose—if they wanted to, they could open the little building and find out what was inside."

Larry was impressed. He had thought the man's story would turn out to be either something simple like getting caught in a combine, or a wholesale whopper like a great white whale. He definitely felt he was getting his bought beer's worth.

"Now," said the man, "there was a man with McCabe, a Polynesian man named... ah, I've forgotten his name. Anyway, he was an Islander, and when they saw the little building he hung back outside the wall, and when McCabe started messing with the bricks, he told him to leave it alone. He said, 'The old people went to a lot of trouble to wall up that door—why do you want to undo their hard work?' McCabe just laughed and called him superstitious, and the other men laughed too, and those who hadn't really cared what was inside now wanted to, to prove they weren't superstitious too."

Chuck said, "Last call, fellas." The man still had half his beer left, and Larry didn't feel like another, so he just shook his head slightly at Chuck.

"It's that late?" said the man. "I'll need to get along pretty soon."

"Oh, we've got a couple of minutes," Larry said. "And you really can't stop now, right? I'm hooked!"

The man smiled at Larry and looked him up and down with his one good eye, then took a swallow of his beer before continuing.

"So the men made a human chain, with McCabe pulling out the loose bricks from the doorway, and the rest handing them along to dump them over the wall out of the way. And when they got most of the bricks out of the doorway, McCabe leaned in so he could see, and you know what he saw? A skeleton."

The man coughed, and took another swig of his beer to clear his throat. Larry could feel the pressure from the evening's beers on his bladder, but he didn't want to pause the story for a trip to the men's room; who knew if the man would ever get started again?

"It was green, moss green like the bricks, from sitting in the jungle for hundreds of years," the man said. "Some bones were missing, but most were there. And the skull... its teeth... were pointed. All of them. Like two rows of needles."

Suddenly the man glanced up. "Hell, is that the time?" He put both hands against the bar and swiveled the stool towards his crutch. "Got to catch my bus."

"Wait!" said Larry, jumping down from his stool. There were only a couple of regulars left in the place, finishing up their beers. Chuck leaned against the end of the bar near the door, watching people exit.

The man wedged his crutch beneath his arm and hopped toward the door. "If I miss my bus, I'll be stuck on the streets all night, you know."

"But—I—Here, let me help you to the bus stop." Larry almost grabbed the man's arm to usher him out. "And you can finish your story."

The door jingled as they exited, and the cold, silent breath of night air was like a slap in Larry's face. He felt his bladder contract and wished he had found some juncture at which to relieve himself earlier. The bar was two steps down from the street, and he helped the man up to sidewalk level. With his free hand, the man pointed right, and Larry walked alongside him, trying to appear helpful.

"So, the skeleton," Larry prodded.

"Yes, the skeleton," said the man. "Did I tell you about the teeth? Pointed."

"Yes. Pointed teeth. And then?"

The end of the crutch made a hard, brittle sound on the side-walk as the man hop-stepped, in contrast the the shuffle of his lone shoe.

"This man McCabe picked up the skull," the man said. He was moving at a fair pace, but his voice wasn't winded. "He was just as spooked as the rest of them, all right, but he didn't want to let on. So he went for bravado. He picked up the skull with the jawbone and held them like a puppet. 'Hello, mates,' he said in a high voice, just like that. 'Good of you to drop in!' He hoped that his friends would laugh and it would break the tension, but they just stared at him, like he had pissed on a cross."

The island of light around The Drowned Out was receding be-hind them, and the nearest streetlight seemed impossibly distant. Larry found it hard to keep up with the man, much less render any aid. He gave up the pretext and trotted alongside him.

"The old bones were slick with moss," the man said. "McCabe's hand slipped while he was handling them, and his thumb landed on one of the teeth. It was still sharp as a pin, and it poked him and drew blood."

The man halted, and Larry almost tripped over the crutch as he stopped short. They seemed to be halfway between the bar and the streetlight—was that where the bus stop was?—and the man was nothing but a silhouette in the darkness.

The man laughed then, low and moist and throaty. Larry's pulse had already been high from the chill and the walk; now it leaped upward again.

"And?" said Larry. "And? How does it end?"

"They all died."

Larry fluttered his hands in confusion. "Wait—what? That can't be—that's a dumb ending, McCabe! And it doesn't even tell me how you lost your—"

The man leaned in. "'McCabe'? I'm not McCabe. Not much of me, anyway. And I did tell you how I lost it. Most of the bones were there, I said. Most. But not all."

The man leaned in closer, his mouth still open in silent laughter, open wide enough that Larry could see his long green teeth, like a mouthful of needles.

The Straightest Road in Maine

So it's night, black night, not even the moon is out, and we're driv-ing a road that cuts through the pines on either side and not a house anywhere. Every once in a while I see the light from a house far back in the trees, but I can't tell for the life of me how you'd get to one of them because there hasn't been a crossroads or a fork or even a driveway for miles and miles. Not that I want to turn, this is the road I want, but still, how do people get to their homes? Hell, why do they live here in the first place?

Mary is in the passenger seat and I hate to glance over to her be-cause everything that's wrong with her now is right in her profile. Nose is still cute, sure, but under her chin I can see all the stuff that wasn't there before she had kids, and that always reminds me of what's under her coat, hanging over her belt. After the kids were born I said, Better exercise and do something about that or it won't stay empty, it'll fill in with fat, but she didn't appreciate me saying that and didn't exercise and what do you know, what I said hap-pened. I think she did it just to spite me or something, because honestly, who'd *want* to look that way? Sure, I got more pounds on me than I had when we got married but men carry it better.

And it doesn't help things that Mindy is in the back seat, Mary's kid sister, and she leans forward between the front bucket seats to see the road and talk to us when we talk. She's got a perfect set of knockers, better than Mary's ever were even before she started squeezing out babies and her boobs inflated and deflated and inflated and deflated until they look like old pillows, and when Mindy leans forward toward us the V-neck of her shirt lets you see all the way to Florida. I adjusted the rearview mirror so I could see better because, hey, just because you've bought a horse doesn't mean you have to close your eyes when you pass a stable, right? And anyway, it's not like there's anything else to see out here, the road goes straight in front of the headlights and disappears into the dark and there's nothing but night further on and to the sides and behind us. That's why I'm okay with twisting the rearview mirror to check out Mindy because it's not like there's anything behind us, hasn't been for probably an hour, and anyway that's what side mirrors are for.

Mary says, Keep your eyes on the road, almost like she knows what I'm looking at, but she can't because she's just staring straight ahead, has been all the way up from New Hampshire. Mindy's got a job in Maine at some resort that wants her there this early in the spring to help them get ready and she doesn't have a car, so we're driving her up to drop her off until October. Nothing good on the radio, and Mary doesn't say anything except stuff like *Keep your eyes on the road*, and Mindy's a hottie but she's dumber than hell, so it's been a long silent ride.

Mary says, Do you think we're lost? And I say, How the hell could we be lost? We were on the right road leaving Bangor, and there's been nowhere to get lost since. This has got to be the straightest road in Maine, and there aren't any signs because there don't need to be, there are no frigging decisions to make while you drive, just keep going straight and sooner or later you'll get where you're trying to go. And anyway, even if we were lost, and Mary says, Okay, fine, but I'm still talking, Even if we were lost, who would we stop and ask? The trees? We haven't passed anything for miles except lights way back in the woods, so when we hit the next gas station, if there is another one before we get where we're going, I'll let you go in and make yourself sure that—

And then something comes out of the dark on the right that looks like a person and right BANG into our grill and Mary screams and Mindy screams and I stomp on the brakes as I hit it and maybe I yell a little too, and the car squeals and spins but stays on the road and we stop, everyone breathing heavy and my hands tight on the wheel and Mindy whimpering, she's hit herself on the seats in front of her because she isn't wearing her seatbelt, and I look at the hood expecting to see a dent and blood but all I see is some straw.

Mary turns to me and starts to say something but I know what she's going to say, that I should get out and see what we hit, and I'd do that anyway so I'm out the door before she says it and my legs are shaky but I walk back toward what we hit. The car is turned a quarter way around so the headlights aren't right back the way we come, but there's enough light to see by. I can see more straw, and a shirt. I get closer and nudge it with my foot, and it takes me a minute to figure out what it is or was: a scarecrow. Straw stuffed into an old shirt, and there are the pants over there.

Who the hell throws a scarecrow out into the middle of the road? I look toward the side of the road where it came from, but I can't see anything that far from the light, and I can't hear anything, and maybe the scarecrow didn't jump out or get thrown out, maybe it was just on the edge of the road and I didn't see it because of bushes or something. I poke at the shirt half of the scarecrow with my foot and I see the sticks inside that held it together, but they aren't sticks, they're bones. I crouch, and I look at the side of the road again, but there's nothing, so I look down and yeah, it's bones. Bones sticking out of the straw. Not fresh bones, old and dry and coming apart, just like the straw is old and moldy and the shirt is falling apart, and I don't know if what I'm seeing are people's bones, they could be from cows or sheep or whatever else they have in Maine, and I really don't want to find out.

I go back to the car, Mindy's still whimpering and rubbing her forehead and Mary's got both hands to her jaw like she does when she's upset. I get in and say, It was just a scarecrow, probably some backwoods idea of a practical joke, and I don't tell them about the bones because it'd just freak them out worse and I don't want to drive the rest of the way with two freaked-out women. Then I say, I guess this is a good time to stop for a leak, anyone who needs to go, but they don't think it's funny, so I put the car in gear and swing around to head back down the road.

And there in front of us is a crowd of men carrying torches, and I slam on my brakes again. I didn't see them come up even though those are frigging torches, but I sure can't miss them now. It looks like thirty of them, and they're dressed all old-timey with beards and broad hats and suspenders, and they all carry torches in one hand and some farming tool in the other—hoes and pitchforks and scythes and things I don't know, nothing like a weedwhacker or anything modern or that takes electricity. And I think, What is this? Because between the scarecrow and all these guys decked out in old-fashioned clothes it seems like a Halloween prank or party or something, and it's the middle of March!

Mary says, Locks the doors! And I do and one older guy walks up to the car. Are they Amish? Does Maine even have Amish? He's got no torch and no pitchfork or whatever, just a cane. He reaches for the door and fumbles with it, like he's never tried to open a car door before, but it's locked anyway.

And I decide I've had enough of this, so I throw it in reverse and turn to look out the back, but now there are farmers behind too, and they have us surrounded. The old guy looks like the leader, and he nods to some of the others, and a guy with a scythe and a guy with a pitchfork attack my back tires and slash them, and another couple do the front. Mary's whimpering just like Mindy now and sniffling some too.

The old guy knocks on the window like it's a front door, and he says, Open, loud enough I can hear it inside. Mary says, Don't! and

Mindy doesn't say anything but she cries louder. And the man says, Open, again, and I just give him the finger. Then he waves to another man to come over, and he's got heavy tool, I don't know what, and he raises it like he's just gonna break in the windshield.

I shout, Hold on! Hold on! I'll open up! and Mary tells me, No! Don't! but it's either that or they keep taking the car apart until they get inside. I unlock the doors and before I can even get out, there are men at every door, opening them and taking the three of us out. They stand us all on one side of the car, side by side, and no one says anything except the one old guy. And he just says, Thank you.

And I say, What the frigging hell are you doing, man? Is this some sort of robbery? You gonna steal the car after you slashed the frigging tires? Is this what you hicks do for kicks, huh? And Mary put her hand on my arm to shut me up, but I don't shut up because what are they going to do that they weren't already going to do?

The old guy just watches my face, all calm-like, until I'm done, like I hadn't just been screaming at him. And then he just says again, Thank you. And I say, For what, huh? For what?

He says, Things need to start growing. It's the season. We need new scarecrows for things to grow. And he waves to some of the men at the back and they come forward with armfuls of loose straw and some rope or twine, and some of the other men put down their tools and take out knives, big butcher knives that look like they've been using them for years and years.

And he says, the old man says, Thank you, again. And all the other men all around us say it together, Thank you. And the men with the knives and the fresh straw come up, and Mindy and Mary start screaming and screaming. And me, I'm screaming too.

In the Plantation House

Finding the plantation house was a blessing from heaven. As the family wearily and silently hauled their wagon down the rutted road, they first saw its roof, a flat line of slate over the kudzu-covered trees, and quickened their plodding steps. When the full house came into view, it was all they could do to keep Little Bee from shouting out loud.

The colonnaded veranda was peeling, and the wooden steps down to what had once been a tended lawn were warped and crumbling, but the walls and the roof still held true. Kudzu covered the windows on the first floor, but hadn't extended to the second or third. Pa motioned Ma to stay with the wagon, and Jacob to pull both of the rifles from the wagon and join him. Unbidden, Robbie followed them, holding his bow at the ready as a rearward. Ma set Eliza, Janice, Little Beatrice and herself each on one side of the wagon to keep watch and raise the alarm if anything moved that wasn't a tree limb in the sluggish breeze.

Pa and Jacob advanced at the ready through the doorless entrance from the warped veranda. They kept their rifles aimed where their eyes tracked, and felt the floorboards cautiously as they stepped. There was furniture in the rooms, some still covered with age-spotted drop cloths, most naked and molested by vermin over the years, but the floor showed no sign of any human tread.

The stairs moaned in protest as they ascended to the second floor, but held solid even when Pa tested each with his whole weight on one foot. The second floor was less disturbed by flora and fauna than the first, and it too showed no sign of occupancy in decades at least. Pa motioned to Jacob and Robbie to check the third floor while he himself examined each of the rooms on the second. He found bed frames with no mattresses, old straight-backed and rocking chairs which held together by sheer Southern obstinacy, and fragments of silvered mirrors in frames warped and flaked by humidity, but no sign that anyone other than themselves was there, or had been, or would be.

Pa, Jacob and Robbie rejoined the womenfolk outside, and Pa gave Ma a long, slow hug. He spoke for the first time that day and said, "Let's move our things in."

While Robbie and Little Bee stood guard on opposite corners of the veranda, the rest hauled their possessions out of the wagon to the second floor. Then, while the womenfolk set to cleaning and arranging some rooms as their living space, Pa and Jacob gathered all of the chairs and slat furniture from all three stories. In a leanto out back Pa found a jar full of rusty nails to supplement his own meager supply, and he and Jacob nailed the wooden furniture into a mass of crosshatched timber and doweling. They threaded a rope through it, pounded a few nails into the ceiling above the second floor landing, and improvised a pulley from a caster off one of the old bed frames. When they were done, they had a light but effective barrier that they could lower into the stairwell, filling and blocking it to anything larger than a cat.

Robbie didn't want to be left to work with the girls but was too small to be much help with the furniture, so Pa set him to his proudest task ever: Robbie was to keep watch from one of the front-facing windows. Pa even set his own rifle against the sill for him to use. "An arrow won't do much good until it's too close," he said. Robbie beamed proudly and stood at attention at the window for hours, intently scanning the environs clear to the road and beyond. Pa didn't tell him that he had unloaded all but one of the precious bullets from the rifle before presenting it to him.

That afternoon, Eliza and Janice explored the rear of the property cautiously and found the well. Its cover was rotted to little more than bark and spongy splinters, but when they had lowered a cooking pot on a rope, they found the water deep and clear. Pa tasted it first, and after his first swallow, he poured the rest of the pot over his head, and allowed himself a true delicacy: a quiet laugh.

That night, Ma and the girls made dinner over the small fire that they kindled in the second-story fireplace with wood that Janice and Little Bee had gathered close around the house, while Robbie and his bow stood guard. The meal was beans once again, and the wearying smell of them cooking, even in the sweet well water, took everyone's quiet exuberance out of them a bit. Sitting on the floor around their meal, they all joined hands and Pa prayed, thanking the Lord for His generosity in helping them find this refuge, and asking that, in the coming days, they would be able to find food to go with the pure water, fruit and vegetable and meat.

That night, the males bundled into one room and the females into another. Pa told them that they didn't even need to set a watch, but he himself got up around moonrise, too nervous to sleep without someone on guard, and stared out the window for hours at the vine-covered trees outlined in moonlight, until the gentle night air and occasional hoot of an owl lulled him back to restfulness.

By design the next day was to be spent lazily, resting tired feet and mending worn clothes before any further repair of the house or exploration of the grounds. In mid-morning Robbie, who was watching at the second-floor window, hissed *Ch-ch*, which was the signal they all used to summon Pa without calling aloud.

Pa came to the window and looked where Robbie pointed. Where the view opened up between the house and the rutted road, one of the dead shambled. Even from this distance, he could tell it was dead; its neck was broken, and its head lay over entirely on its shoulder, bouncing and rolling with each step.

Robbie held up his bow with bright eyes, but Pa shook his head. "I don't doubt your aim, but you know an arrow won't do enough damage," he murmured, not worried that the dead thing would hear him at this distance. "A flesh wound won't kill one of them. It'll only make it interested."

He waved over his back to Jacob, who brought his rifle. "I can shoot, Pa," Jacob said. But Pa shook his head. The bullets were too few to spare for target practice. He motioned both boys away from the window, back toward the doorway where Ma and the girls waited. He steadied the barrel on the window sill, bent to sight with both eyes open, and pulled the trigger.

The bent head jerked wetly, and the dead thing dropped to the road. Before the echoes had even died away, Pa set the rifle down and motioned to Jacob. They pulled up the barrier from the stairwell and charged down.

"At least let me guard from the door," Robbie said, and Pa nodded permission. Robbie stayed on the veranda, his bow at the ready, while Pa and Jacob trotted out toward the road with a shovel. They wrapped handkerchiefs around their faces as they went, but that didn't help much when they got to the body; the bullet had split its soggy skull, and fierce-smelling brain juices formed a splattered puddle in the dust.

Pa held the shovel under one arm, and they each grabbed a leg and dragged as far back up the road as the could, until the leg Jacob held came apart at the knee. They shoved and rolled it to the swampy ditch at the side of the road, and Pa quickly shoveled muck over the body while Jacob looked anxiously up and down the road.

Then Pa want back down the road toward the house, scooping dribbles of rot out of the dust and into the ditch.

"Let's be quick, Pa," Jacob said, trying to sound grown. "You don't know what might have heard that shot."

"I worry about what they smell more than what they hear," Pa said, wiping the sweat from his forehead with his sleeve. "Though how they smell anything over themselves, I don't know."

Once the main splatter of brain had been buried and the shovel wiped on long grass, they made their way back to the house and beyond it. They cleaned off their hands as best they could with well water, then took Robbie with them back to the second floor.

The girls had felt free to hum earlier in the day, but from now until nightfall they had no such urge, and as they held hands again to pray around another dinner of beans, Pa pleaded once more with the Lord for their upkeep, for meat and vegetables, and for safety.

The next day was a rainy Sunday, and Pa insisted they do no work on the Sabbath, not even to strengthen or beautify their new home. He and Ma took turns reading from the Bible, getting through most of The Book of Judges while the children sat against the wall and occasionally nodded.

After the Bible reading and prayer, Ma was just reheating left-over beans for lunch when they heard *Ch-ch*. It was Little Beatrice at the window this time, pointing out toward the road. Pa joined her, followed soon by Robbie, bow in hand.

The drizzling rain had misted the air, and the figure on the road this time wasn't nearly as easy to see—just a silhouette that moved slowly. But Pa could tell where the head was, and that was all he needed. He picked up the rifle leaning beside the window, checked the chamber, and started sighting down the barrel.

"Pa!" whispered Robbie. "It's not dead! Look!"

Pa lowered the rifle and looked again. The figure had taken something from its pocket to look at it. A watch? A compass? Whatever it was, it was an action that none of the dead would make.

"Thank you, son." Pa replaced the rifle against the wall beside the window.

"Pa?" Robbie's face was bright and hopeful.

Pa smiled and nodded.

Robbie raised his bow, steadied it against the window sill, and shot.

The rain got stronger through the day, but never chilled the air beyond comfort. Ma and Eliza discovered only two leaks in the ceiling of the third floor, where they would cause little bother. The dark cloak of rain outside made the house seem separate and safe from the outside world, and everyone napped in the afternoon, even Pa.

And when they sat and joined hands around their supper, Pa once again thanked the Lord for this shelter, and furthermore declared the whole family's gratitude that He had heard their prayers and sent them meat.

Trading With the Ruks

Malachi and his partners met the Ruk caravan at the trading hill outside the village, after a single Ruk, sweating and nervous, had come as herald into the village square to announce their approach and then scrabbled away as fast as his bandy legs could carry him. The hill was far enough away from the village to be hidden by the rolling land, though it was no secret where the village lay; one only had to follow the wagon ruts back from the trading hill, as the lone herald Ruk had done. But mutant tribes were never invited into a village of the Pure, not with rumors and reports of maidens spirited away by various mutant caravans to help keep those deformed races alive.

And then there was the fact that Ruks stank. Malachi steeled himself and kept from flinching as a Ruk from the caravan, evidently its trade captain, climbed to the crest of the trading hill and bowed. He was dressed, like all those in the caravan, in a plain tunic of scavenged fabric that reach to his knobby knees, and as the wind changed, the smell of him caught Malachi like a fist to the side of the head: sour and dank, like wine that had turned to vinegar mixed with mushrooms. Malachi's polite smile never faltered, even as he heard his partners behind him shift and cough.

"Welcome to trade, caravaneer," Malachi said formally. "I am Malachi Asael's son."

"Many thanks for your welcome," the Ruk said. "I am Skuchi Var-Bel Frashaa."

Malachi wondered idly if he had met this particular Ruk at a previous year's trade. He never remembered their names, given only as a formality, and they all looked the same to him: short like a child, with a bald and square head squatting neckless on lumpy shoulders, a pot belly pushing the tunic forward, and spindly arms poking out of the armholes to end in spadelike fingers hanging fully to the knees. This one, this Skuchi, had a necklace of horses' teeth and twisted bits of metal, probably to show his status as chief trader for the caravan. Two of his lieutenants lingered on the slope of the hill; the rest of the Ruks hung back at the bottom with their wagons, their various beasts of burden stomping and whinnying.

Skuchi folded himself to the ground and motioned to his lieutenants, who hurried forward, spread a blanket before him, and dropped several wrapped bundles before retreating. Malachi's men did the same, setting covered baskets before him on the blanket they unrolled.

In a sitting position, Malachi didn't have nearly the advantage of height over the Ruk, and they saw almost eye to eye. Skuchi smiled, showing the gapped, rounded teeth common to all Ruks, and Malachi had a sudden vision of this Ruk or one like it slavering over a winsome maid. He pushed this afterimage of old wives' tales out of his mind.

"Let us trade," Malachi said.

Nothing unexpected was brought to the trading hill today. The Pure had grain and dried beans, cheese, and a few homespun blankets and bolts of cloth. This village was also renowned for having a master flute-maker and his apprentices living and working there, but Malachi knew not to bother bringing those wares up to the trading hill, for they'd only end up carrying them back; of the mutant peoples, only the Glossae had any sense or appreciation of music, and even then their tastes were so alien that only instruments made specifically for Glossae use interested them, and the village flute-maker refused to "profane" his craft to that end.

The Ruks had implements and materials they had scavenged from the dead zones, areas which the Pure wouldn't enter for fear of infertility or mutation. There were metal cooking pots and glass bowls, intact or mostly so; cables of copper and other materials with which the villagers could swap out perishable twine or leather for lashings, and some few garments and footwear, though usable examples of each were getting rarer. There were some ornaments and oddities, but Malachi had learned through hard experience in his early years never to barter for something whose utility wasn't obvious to him, no matter what the Ruks promised.

They shared fresh beer from the village as they traded, and by midday had cleared their wares. Malachi's men loaded foodstuffs which the Ruks had purchased over to their caravan, and the Ruks filled the villagers' empty wagons, though not wholly, with the wares that Malachi had bargained for.

At last Malachi got stiffly to his feet as his men cleaned up his blanket. His lower back ached, and his head thumped with the heat of the sunlight and the beer. Skuchi hopped up like a frog.

"It is always a pleasure, Malachi," the Ruk said. "These many years, you have been a fair and friendly partner in trade."

At least the Ruks can tell *us* apart, Malachi thought. "I am honored," Malachi replied. "And I always look forward to your appearance in trading season." The heat of the sun had not improved the Ruk's stench, and Malachi wished that the wind would change.

Skuchi glanced behind Malachi to where his men were securing their purchases down to the wagons. "I have something for you, as one of our favorite traders," he said in a lower voice. "I did not bring it out earlier, because I didn't want it to become an item of trade. It is a gift."

"Really?" Malachi was too late in hiding his surprise. Ruks were known for being forthright traders, not for their generosity. The last of the beer had been drunk an hour before, and Malachi's mouth was coated with dry stickiness.

"Please, keep this to yourself," Skuchi said, holding up a broad-fingered hand. "We Ruks have a reputation to uphold. Is there any way you can dismiss your men without arousing suspicion?"

Malachi's chest puffed up. He had already been steeling himself for a week of muttered complaints from those who thought that he hadn't gained as much advantage in the trade as they thought reasonable. Not that any of *them* volunteered for the duty, no; they just assumed from their comfortable homes that they would trade more keenly with the stinking Ruks. At least *someone* appreciated his efforts at barter, and if it wasn't one of the Pure, well, a gift was a gift.

Malachi descended the hill halfway and called to his men, "Ho! The Ruks want me to help them with their maps! Go on without me!"

The men signaled assent, and Malachi returned to where Skuchi was waiting. "Come," Skuchi said, "we have kept it at the caravan."

Malachi followed the trollish mutant down the side of his hill, realizing with a start that he was going to be closer to the Ruk caravan, and to more than a single Ruk at a time, than he had ever been. The various wagons of the caravan were moving into single file for travel, their beasts of burdens as varied as the vehicles they pulled: open wagons, two-wheeled carts, wagons with fabric tents suspended above, and some which were like boxes on wheels, constructed of scavenged wood. The air got thicker with Ruk-stench as they came among the wagons, and Malachi found that even breathing through his mouth didn't help overmuch; instead, he fancied he could taste the stink.

Following Skuchi, he rounded a wagon which was wholly enclosed, with window spaces and a low doorway covered with shutters that barred from the outside. He half-wondered idly if locked wagons like this contributed to the tales of Ruk-abducted maidens; then he saw something out of the corner of his eye, something aimed toward his head. It struck before he could defend himself, and the world whirled into haze and blackness.

Malachi only realized that he was approaching consciousness again because of the smell. He had thought he knew how bad Ruk-smell could be, but wherever he was now, the stink in his nostrils was so thick it almost choked the air from his lungs. He was afraid to open his eyes because the smell might actually be thick enough to see.

He shifted his arms, intending to cradle his aching head, but his arms wouldn't move; they were held out away from his body by something tied around his wrists. His ankles, too, were held immobile, spread apart from each other. His eyes opened, despite the promised pain when he did so, and he found himself in a small boxlike space, dark except by dim light creeping between ill-fitting boards. The floor of the box was covered with filthy straw; his arms and legs were gripped by manacles of materials from the Long Ago, metal and wire cobbled together.

As his vision cleared gradually, he looked again at the space that held him, at the shuttered windows and low door, and realized that he was inside the wagon he had noticed right before— before what? Before he was attacked, obviously. But why?

The door at the far end opened. Beyond it was night, with the glare of an unseen fire reflecting inside; he had obviously been unconscious for hours, long enough for the caravan to have moved far from the village. How long before anyone had become suspicious that his return from trading was taking so long?

The doorway was filled with the silhouette of a Ruk who clambered inside. The door was closed from without, and Malachi could hear the bar dropping. Then the Ruk uncovered a lantern, and the yellow light fell upon a necklace of horses' teeth and metal around the Ruk's neck.

"I'm glad to see you awake," Skuchi said. "I had half-feared that I had struck you too hard."

"S... Skuchi?" Malachi mumbled, finding that his mouth was

still sluggish.

"At last, you remember me!" Skuchi said, mouth distended in a wide, grotesque smile. "Every year, I can tell that I am new to you. Perhaps all Ruks look alike to you, heh?"

In his other hand, Skuchi held a small box made from more materials from Long Ago. He reached it out with his long spidery arms and flipped it open with a blunt thumb. Malachi couldn't see what was inside it, but vapors fairly leapt out, a different smell that was piercing instead of cloying, sharp instead of bludgeoning. Malachi felt a wave of dizziness and heard his blood pounding in his temples, his neck, his loins, his whole body. Skuchi flipped the box closed, and Malachi lay there with his breath coming in gasps, his heart thumping, sweat starting out all over his body.

Skuchi set the box and the lantern down in the far corner of the wagon. "You are one of our favorite traders," he crooned, "certainly *my* favorite trader. And this is how we show our favor."

With both hands he lifted the lower edge of his tunic. Unable to look away, Malachi saw the protruding belly exposed, and beneath it, where he had expected to see a mutated version of his own manhood... he saw nothing.

And against his will he understood.

Skuchi held the tunic up beneath his—beneath *her* arms. "You have much we will take in trade, my sisters and I," she chuckled.

Malachi was gasping too convulsively even to scream.

Wait

The doctor's waiting room smell like toilet bowl cleaner. Meredith sat uncomfortably in a chair molded from plastic, cushioned with a thin layer of synthetic rust-colored material the texture of burlap and bolted to three identical chairs before the row was broken by a featureless table on which were strewn a handful of magazines. There were more seats beyond that, and an identical arrangement on the opposite side of the room. The hands of the clock on the far wall said 10:24 A.M.

She had no intention of touching the magazines, all of which looked well-thumbed and at least two months old. Handling the pages that had been groped for weeks by the sweaty, coughed-upon hands of sick people... The idea gave her a queasy shudder in her abdomen. She had no reading material with her, and there was no TV or radio in the waiting room. She stared at her fingernails. They weren't very entertaining.

On the other side of the magazine table sat an old man in black cargo pants and a black safari jacket. His arms were crossed over his stomach and he leaned forward, rocking slightly. Meredith hoped those weren't the signs of nausea. He was more than old, she realized; he was *very* old. The hair sprouting from his ears was almost thicker than the few strands stubbornly clinging to his spotty scalp, and his eyes were lost in a corduroy sea of wrinkles. His lips were moving but made no sound.

Across from Meredith sat a chubby woman with an infant in her arms, swaddled so completely it might have been wearing a baby burqa. The woman was peering into the blanketed bundle, her unconscious smile waxing and waning. Some people are endlessly fascinated by their own offspring. Meredith had no children, so she didn't know if she was one of those people, but she suspected she was not. Still, a baby had to be more interesting than fingernails.

The thin older lady in the far corner of the room was the only one browsing a magazine, although from the severe way she flipped the pages she seemed more to be judging the contents and finding them wanting. Her squarish glasses were the size of cathode ray tubes, her makeup was precise and meticulous, and her hair was dyed strawberry blonde to hide the gray and hairsprayed back into a simple straight style. For a moment, Meredith entertained the notion that it was actually the woman's hair that smelled like toilet cleaner.

The only sounds in the room were the constant electrical hum of the clock and the fluorescent lights, and breathing: the old man's shallow breaths punctuated by the consonants of his silent monologue, the wordless cooing of the chubby woman to her baby, the dismissive snort from the thin woman's nose as she flipped the pages of the magazine. Meredith couldn't hear her own breath along with the other three occupants in the room; was she really that silent a breather? Or do people learn to tune out the sound of their own breath? Experimentally she inhaled more deeply, and was rewarded with the soft *whish* of air passing up her nostrils, and a tickle of dust. She rubbed her nose with the back of her hand and set it back in her lap.

The old man's rocking back and forth was becoming more animated, and Meredith almost caught what he was muttering to himself. If he was in as much distress as it looked like, he should probably have gone to the hospital instead of the doctor's office. She couldn't make out what he was saying, but it sounded repetitive, like a mantra or prayer.

The door at the far end of the waiting room opened, and the nurse filled it. She was a tall woman, probably quite comely before her lower half had expanded with age. She was dressed in one of the cartoon-pattern scrub shirts that all the medical personnel wear nowadays. She looked at her clipboard and said, "Mr. Lancaster?"

The old man rocked onto his feet and stumbled toward the door, his arms still clasped across his stomach. The nurse put her arm around his shoulder to guide him as he stepped into the back. The door clicked shut, and the almost-silence resumed.

Meredith glanced to where he had been sitting and was shocked to see dark wetness spreading on the rust-colored upholstery of the backrest and seat. She glanced at the chubby woman and the thin lady, but neither of them were looking the right direction to see it.

Meredith got up and went to the reception counter beside the door into the back office. She could only see the girl sitting behind the counter when she was standing right at it. The girl had dark ringleted hair, and wore bright and feminine makeup like an old-style pinup. She was pretty enough to be a pinup, too, except for her crooked and yellowed teeth which showed when she was smiling, and she was always smiling. She looked up eagerly as Meredith approached.

"Um," said Meredith, "that man who just went in, I think he was injured and leaked on... There's a spot..." she pointed back toward the chair.

The receptionist smiled and nodded as is she had expected the news. "I'll send someone out to take care of it right away."

"Great. Just... thought you should know."

She stepped back, and the receptionist was swallowed up behind the counter. As she turned to make her way back to her seat, the thin lady looked up from her magazine and stared at her through her enormous glasses.

"They won't let you out, you know," she said in the voice Meredith imagined she'd use with a naughty child that she didn't particularly like.

"Excuse me?" Meredith said, but the lady had already gone back to her magazine, flipping the pages with a dissatisfied snort. Meredith looked back at her once when she got back to her own seat.

The clock now said 10:27 A.M. Only that much time had passed? Meredith slumped in her seat. Doctor's offices were a near-perfect mixture of anxiety and boredom. She clasped her hands on her stomach and actually twiddled her thumbs.

The chubby woman was still whispering and cooing to her bundled-up baby, and the baby was mewing back. Mewing? Meredith stilled even her silent breath to listen more intently. Yes, mewing. The baby didn't make much sound, but when it did it sounded more like a kitten than a human. At least it wasn't crying; being stuck in this otherwise-quiet room with a crying baby would do things to her nerves.

The outside door opened, and a man with two weeks' beard came in carrying a metal utility case. He looked at the empty chairs around the room, then centered on the dark splotch on the old man's seat.

He knelt in front of the seat and set his utility case to the side. Meredith watched, not so much because cleaning was so interesting but because he was the only thing moving in the room. He got down on the level of the seat and stared at the spot. Then he opened his case and pulled out a cotton swab and a clear plastic tube. He brushed the swab gently across the spot and held it up. The head of the swab was stained red.

He dropped the swab into the tube and screwed its lid on, then dropped the tube back into the case. He snapped the catches on the case shut, hopped to his knees, and left the office. Meredith watched him go and heard his footsteps disappear down the hall. She turned back to the dark spot. She felt like moving over another seat, away from the bloody blotch.

She sighed, leaned her head back against the wall, and looked again at the chubby woman. It took her a few seconds to realize that there was something different about her face. Along her jawline, just to the left of her chin, was a small bloody scratch. More than one scratch, actually, in parallel. It hadn't been there before. The woman didn't seem upset by it, but Meredith couldn't look away as a slow bead of blood formed along the deepest scratch.

The woman burbled into her baby bundle. Then she leaned her face down into the wrapped blankets, chin first. Meredith was almost sure she heard sucking sounds. When the woman raised her face again, the blood was gone, and the area around the scratches was moist.

The maintenance man re-entered while Meredith was staring at the woman. In a repeat of his last visit, he crossed to the stained seat, knelt in front of it, and swabbed it. He left again with his bloody swab in his case. Meredith was still listening to his vanishing footsteps when she heard the office door open behind her.

The nurse leaned out. She had changed her scrub shirt, Meredith noticed; this one was in a Hawaiian pattern, with bright fruit standing out against dark green palm trees.

"Mrs. Hallam?" the nurse said, and the chubby woman stood up with her baby. She looked into the blankets the whole time she was crossing the floor, and she and the nurse giggled to one another. Meredith could hear them start talking as the door swung closed. The only words she thought she heard were "the claw." Or maybe it was "de-claw."

Meredith's eyes drifted from the door, and she started when she saw the thin lady's stare hard upon her, magnified by her huge square glasses.

"I didn't give them my name," the lady said, "but it won't matter, you'll see. You didn't think they'd let you leave, did you? Did you?"

Meredith had no answer. She grimaced in discomfort, and tried to think of some way to end the conversation—though it wasn't much of a dialog—without being obviously rude.

"You haven't been watching," the lady continued. "Not watching the right things. You haven't seen the signs." She tossed her magazine aside on the empty seat beside her. "The hands on the clock are the only ones they leave behind, you know. And they like the stains."

The stains. Meredith looked at the dark splotch. A fly was crawling across it, sampling it. Meredith felt her stomach roll. She smiled politely to the lady, then stood up and crossed again to the reception counter. The girl behind it smiled at her as before. Meredith could see her makeup was too thick; the foundation was starting to show cracks at the corners of her mouth and eyes.

"I'm sorry, but that spot on the chair," Meredith said. "Someone's been in here twice now—the custodian, I suppose—but he hasn't cleaned it up, or even done anything to cover it. I really don't think it's sanitary, leaving it like that."

The girl smiled and nodded as she had before. "I'll send someone out to take care of it right away." Her lips didn't move when she spoke, but her tongue wriggled behind her twisted teeth.

Meredith didn't feel anything had been resolved, but she was even more uncomfortable standing here than sitting. Still, there was nothing forcing her to sit close to the fouled seat. She walked past the thin lady who was now sitting with her hands primly on her knees and instead seated herself on the bank of chairs that the chubby woman had vacated. Not in the same seat, though. There was something left behind on that seat, and it took Meredith a moment's attention to identify it: it had been a baby's pacifier, but the soft nipple was torn away, the edge of the rubber shredded as if it had gone through a meat grinder.

The door opened again, and the custodian entered for a third time. He held the door for a larger man dressed in khaki and denim. The larger man held the utility case this time. He stopped just inside the door and scanned the room with bulbous, unblinking eyes. He had a short, squat nose, and cheeks pitted with acne scars. Meredith looked away when his eyes fell upon her.

The custodian from earlier gestured wordlessly to the stained seat. The larger man—his boss, maybe? His supervisor?—went to the seat and knelt on the carpet, setting the case beside him. The smaller custodian knelt a pace behind him. The supervisor didn't open his case. He leaned his elbows on the edge of the seat. Then he extended his right hand to the back of the seat, trailed three fingers down the bloody wetness, and brought them to his face.

Meredith grimaced and turned her head away. The thin lady was watching her, ignoring the two custodians. Meredith was afraid to look back, afraid that the two men were also watching her too, but the lady's glare was too hard to endure. But when she turned her head back, the custodians weren't watching her. Instead they had gotten to their feet, and now both of them left, the smaller again holding the door for the latter. On the larger man's face were three parallel stripes in watery red, extending from his hairline down onto his cheeks and the bridge of his nose. The stain was still there on the chair, but now there was something else too: a tooth. It looked human. The fly buzzed through the air and landed on the tooth to examine it with its forelegs.

The door to the back office opened, and the nurse stepped halfway out. She had changed her shirt again; this one was still tropical themed, green palm trees against a black background, but mixed among the trees were white skulls with open mouths and snaking red tongues.

"Ma'am?" she said, looking toward the thin lady, who was still staring hard at Meredith.

"I didn't tell them my name," she said, her voice now despairing. "But that doesn't help any. You see?"

"Ma'am." The nurse motioned with her clipboard. Reluctantly, the thin lady stood up. She was shorter than Meredith had thought, almost childlike in her proportions, and the nurse towered over her as she ushered her into the back and closed the door. From where she was now sitting, Meredith caught a glimpse of the office behind the door. It was black—not unlit, but painted black.

Now she was alone in the waiting room, alone with the hum of the lights and the clock. There was no breathing, not even her own.

She turned in her seat and craned to see the clock, which was now above and behind her. It read 10:31 A.M.

She stood up and went to the reception counter.

"I think your clock is falling behind," she said. "It's moving awfully slowly."

The girl smiled at her, and Meredith saw that the cracks weren't in her makeup after all; they were in her face. Her entire pinup's face was slowly detaching, cracks and creases spreading across it like brittle wax.

"I'll send someone out to take care of it right away," she said. Her wax face didn't move at all. Meredith could see her tongue thrashing behind the twisted teeth, translucent and segmented like a maggot.

"Do you know what time it is?" Meredith asked.

"I'll send someone out to take care of it right away," the girl answered. She raised a hand slowly and pointed back to where Meredith had been sitting.

Meredith returned to her seat and huddled there.

No one who had gone into the office had come out.

To keep herself from standing and pacing, she finally reached to the low table and pulled over the first magazine she touched. Its name, *Sporting Review*, was the only thing she could read on the cover; the rest of the type was in some language she didn't understand or even recognize. The characters were rounded, stylized pictograms that reminded her of pictures of embryos. The figure on the cover was a smiling man, bronzed skinned and black haired, standing in a stone arena, dressed in nothing but a loin clothing and a feathered head band. His number, 21, was painted on his bare chest with white paint. He proudly held aloft the head of a defeated competitor.

Meredith pushed the magazine back without opening it and looked at the clock again. It still read 10:31 A.M. The fly on the stained seat had taken to the air and now flew in crazy circles around the room, its drone mixing with the sound of the lights and the clock.

The office door opened, and the nurse stood there. Her shirt now was pure black, with a single white skull in the center of her chest, its lascivious red tongue looping out and down and around.

"Meredith," she said.

Meredith glanced back at the clock. 10:31 A.M., now and for-ever.

"Meredith," the nurse repeated.

Her stomach tied itself in knots. She looked at her fingernails, not wanting to meet the nurse's eyes.

"Meredith," the nurse said firmly. "The doctor will see you now."

Credits and Acknowledgments

"Party Favors" first appeared in the Fall 1990 issue of *Amazing Stories*, under the byline "Alex Nathan Shumate."

"Other Duties" first appeared in *Mormons & Monsters*, edited by Wm Morris and Theric Johnson.

"Trading With the Ruks" first appeared in *Finding Home: Community in Apocalyptic Worlds*, edited by Caroline Dombrowski.

All other stories are published here for the first time.

The majority of the stories in this volume—"Somewhere in Nebraska or Maybe Colorado," "Bookmobile Day," "An Eldritch Correspondence," "Forbidden Aisles," "Love Among the Kryil," "The Night Children," "On the Demise of Rory Calloran," "Story in a Bar," "The Straightest Road in Maine," "In the Plantation House," "Trading With the Ruks," and "Wait"—had their genesis in a single month. My friend Dan Wells (author of the *I Am Not a Serial Killer* books and the *Partials* series) had proposed doing a "NaShoStoMo" challenge, writing a new short story every day for a month. That fired my enthusiasm, so in April 2011, I wrote the first drafts of thirty short stories. Some were little more than vignettes, and others were shoddy piffle whose only purpose was to fulfill the letter of the challenge, but right between the fourteenth and twenty-first days I hit a sweet spot, and the result was most of those NaShoSto-Mo stories included here. I highly recommend the exercise. (Ironically, Dan was unable to participate because of a book tour, and hasn't yet, to my knowledge, taken the challenge that he first proposed.)

If you enjoyed this book, check out some of the other publications from Cold Fusion Media:

Shared Nightmares
Edited by Steven Diamond and Nathan Shumate

Twelve authors— including New York Times bestseller Larry Correia, #1 Amazon bestseller Michaelbrent Collings, Prometheus Award winner Sarah Hoyt, Campbell Award nominee Max Gladstone, and Hugo nominee Howard Tayler—take you to the dark side of the dream world, where phantasms and fears become frighteningly real.

Space Eldritch

Science fiction goes occult in *Space Eldritch*, a volume of seven original novelettes and novellas of Lovecraftian pulp space opera. Featuring work by Brad R. Torgersen (Hugo/Nebula/Campbell nominee), Howard Tayler (multiple Hugo nominee), and Michael R. Collings (author of over 100 books), plus a foreword by New York Times bestselling author Larry Correia, *Space Eldritch* inhabits the intersection between the eternal adventure of the

final frontier and the inhuman darkness between the stars.

Space Eldritch II: The Haunted Stars

The cold of interstellar space is again closer than you think as eleven authors—including New York Times bestseller Larry Correia, Nebula winner Eric James Stone, Amazon #1 bestseller Michaelbrent Collings, and multiple Hugo nominee Howard Tayler—explore what happens when space opera meets Lovecraftian cosmic horror.

Arcane Sampler
Edited by Nathan Shumate

A bite-sized collection featuring twelve unsettling original stories, *Arcane Sampler* demonstrates the kind of macabre storytelling that characterizes the *Arcane* series of anthologies — for only 99 cents! Included:

- The performers in a traveling carnival suddenly find themselves in mortal danger from their latest exhibit...
- A Bible salesman discovers a reclusive family who worships something older... and closer...
- A good Samaritan stopping to give roadside assistance encounters something far more dangerous than a flat tire...

Arcane
Edited by Nathan Shumate

The first full-length anthology of this series features thirty stories by some of the freshest blood in the horror, dark fantasy and weird fiction fields! Included:

- An office worker returns from bereavement leave to find his workplace changing before his eyes...
- A priest excites his village to the greatest show of devotion to their god ever seen...
- A mortician sees all of his immaculate handiwork destroyed when his clients start rising...

Arcane II
Edited by Nathan Shumate

This second volume of the *Arcane* anthology series presents twenty-one more stories of dark imagination. Included:

- A landlord finds something left behind by a former tenant, something with a will of its own...
- A bride explores her new husband's manor house, seeking the mystery that overshadows his life...
- A survivor of the apocalypse sees an insidious change infecting the few remaining humans...

The Golden Age of Crap
by Nathan Shumate

Just because you can't respect a movie doesn't mean you can't enjoy it. *The Golden Age of Crap* serves up a sampling of junk-food flicks that gained their audiences on videocassette rental shelves during the '80s and '90s, a time when one couldn't visit the video rental store without being tempted by Italian post-apocalyptic adventures, ninja revenge yarns, and zombie-filled "camcorder epics." The movies covered here run from sleeper hits (*Phantasm II*) to cult favorites (*The Dead Next Door*), from unknown stinkers (*Plutonium Baby*) to undiscovered gems (*America's Deadliest Home Video*), all examined with a critical but fun-loving eye.

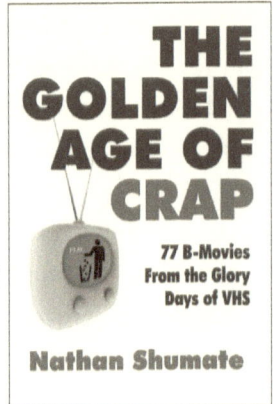

Cold Fusion Media
http://www.coldfusionmedia.us

www.ingramcontent.com/pod-product-compliance
Lightning Source LLC
Chambersburg PA
CBHW020417150626
46554CB00014B/1909